THE FOUR4H DOOR

THE
Four4h
Door

Paul Halter

TRANSLATED BY TOM MEAD

First published as *La Quatrième Porte* in 1987 by Librairie des Champs-Élysées, Paris

This paperback translation published in the UK in 2025 by No Exit Press,
an imprint of Bedford Square Publishers Ltd,
London, UK

noexit.co.uk
@noexitpress

© Paul Halter, 2025
This English translation © Tom Mead, 2025
A Maxim Jakubowski book

The right of Paul Halter to be identified as the author of this work has been asserted in accordance with the Copyright, Designs and Patents Act 1988. All rights reserved. No part of this book may be reproduced, stored in or introduced into a retrieval system, or transmitted, in any form or by any means (electronic, mechanical, photocopying, recording or otherwise) without the written permission of the publishers.

Any person who does any unauthorised act in relation to this publication may be liable to criminal prosecution and civil claims for damages.
A CIP catalogue record for this book is available from the British Library.
This is a work of fiction. Names, characters, places, and incidents either are the product of the author's imagination or are used fictitiously, and any resemblance to actual persons, living or dead, businesses, companies, events or locales is entirely coincidental.

ISBN
978-1-83501-348-9 (Paperback)
978-1-83501-349-6 (eBook)

2 4 6 8 10 9 7 5 3 1

Typeset in 11.25 on 14pt Garamond MT Pro
by Avocet Typeset, Bideford, Devon, EX39 2BP
Printed and bound in Great Britain by
CPI Group (UK) Ltd, Croydon CR0 4YY

The manufacturer's authorised representative in the EU for product safety is Easy Access System Europe, Mustamäe tee 50, 10621 Tallinn, Estonia
gpsr.requests@easproject.com

All my thanks to Roland Lacourbe, whose *Houdini et sa légende* (Éditions Techniques du Spectacle Strasbourg) I cheerfully plundered for certain historical elements of this novel.
PH

Contents

CAST OF CHARACTERS — 8

PART ONE — 9
1: A LIGHT IN THE DARKNESS — 11
2: NIGHTMARE — 19
3: A SINGULAR SUICIDE — 28
4: A LETTER TO LOUISE — 36
5: A VISIT FROM THE DEAD — 49
6: A FRENZIED ATTACK — 56
7: THE GIFT OF UBIQUITY — 60

PART TWO — 65
1: A DANGEROUS ENCOUNTER — 67
2: THE HAUNTED ROOM — 73
3: LOSING OUR MINDS — 83
4: AN AUDIENCE WITH THE PSYCHOLOGIST — 93
5: AN IMPOSSIBLE CRIME — 114
6: WHODUNIT? — 127

PART THREE — 143
ENTR'ACTE — 145

PART FOUR — 153
1: EXPLANATIONS — 155
2: THE PSYCHOLOGIST LOSES HIS MIND — 170
3: LAST RESPECTS — 175

PART FIVE — 179
EPILOGUE — 181

CAST OF CHARACTERS

James Stevens
Narrator, a student

Elizabeth Stevens
His sister

Henry White
Friend and neighbour of James Stevens

Arthur White
Henry's father, an author

John Darnley
Friend and neighbour of James Stevens

Victor Darnley
John's father

Alice and Patrick Latimer
Victor Darnley's tenants

Ronald Bowers
Mystery novelist

Dr Alan Twist
Criminologist

PART ONE

1

A LIGHT IN THE DARKNESS

I HAD GONE TO BED EARLY THAT evening, planning to read for a while. No sooner had I settled down than I heard three sharp knocks at my door. It was my sister Elizabeth – she certainly knew how to pick her moments.

At eighteen she was a beautiful young woman, though I doubt she was aware of the fact. She'd changed a great deal recently. Her looks had not gone unnoticed by John Darnley, who doggedly pursued her. Elizabeth was flattered, of course, but her heart was set on my neighbour and closest friend, Henry White. Usually a confident sort, Henry was curiously shy around young women, and Elizabeth in particular; Elizabeth, with whom he was quite obviously besotted.

'I'm not bothering you, am I, James?' she asked, her hand still resting on the door handle.

'Of course not,' I sighed, nose buried in my book.

She sat next to me on the bed, hanging her head and wringing her hands anxiously, before turning to face me with a look of the utmost seriousness in her big dark eyes:

'James, I need to talk to you.'

'All right.'

'It's about Henry.'

'Ah.'

I knew what was coming: I was going to have to act as go-between for a pair of young lovers too proud and too timid to show their true feelings.

Elizabeth snatched the book from my hands and snapped, 'Are you listening, James?'

Startled – my sister seldom raised her voice – I gave her a quick glance. Then I lit a cigarette with calculated slowness and plumed a few smoke rings. When we were small, I used to love making her angry by keeping quiet and feigning indifference to her tantrums, which inevitably plunged her into a blind fury. I must admit that I hadn't lost this annoying habit. However, not wanting to push her too far, I gave in:

'I'm listening.'

'It's about Henry. He…'

'About Henry,' I echoed, looking interested (disbelief flickered in her eyes). 'One moment, please…'

I got up, went over to my bookshelf, grabbed the first volume of an encyclopedia, which I propped open on my lap, before declaring ironically:

'Since you like talking about him so much, and since I find it all so terribly interesting, I've written a modest monograph on the subject. It's eight-hundred pages; this is the first volume…'

I thought she was going to choke with rage. She bolted for the door, but I blocked her path. It took five solid minutes to calm her down.

'All right, I'm all ears. You can count on your big brother.' (I was just over a year older than her.) 'I'll sort it out for you.'

She took a deep breath and confided:

'I'm in love with Henry.'

'I'm aware of that.'

'Henry's in love with me.'

'I'm aware of that too.'

'But he's too shy to do anything about it.'

'Give it some time, you'll see…'

'I shouldn't have to make the first move. That's not my style. Do I seem like one of those girls? He might take me for some sort of…'

'No, no, and no, there's certainly no question of that.'

She wiped her eyes in angry silence before continuing:

'Three days ago, I thought he was going to kiss me. We were walking along the path that leads to the woods, it was getting dark and I said I was cold. He put his arm around me and we walked on in silence. Then he leaned in close; he was about to kiss me – I swear he was, James – the look in his eyes gave him away. Suddenly he bent down and picked up an old piece of string which was lying on the ground, exclaiming: "Look, look at what I can do, Elizabeth!" Then he tied some knots in the string.'

'And?'

'Then,' she said, fighting back tears, 'he took off his shoes and…'

'And?'

'And his socks…'

'Oh, Elizabeth. Don't tell me. Let me guess: he undid the knots with his toes?'

'Exactly,' Elizabeth lamented, 'all thoughts of kissing me were gone.'

'Ha! That sounds like good old Henry all right.'

'I don't happen to find it particularly funny.'

'Come on, sis, can't you see he was trying to amuse you? To entertain you? Even – dare I say it – to *woo* you? That's just his way…'

'Well, I'd much rather he kissed me!' she sulked.

An unusual fellow, that Henry. He'd been a little *different* from the day he was born – prematurely, as it happens. Not that this held him back in any way; his mother lavished him with plenty of loving care as he was growing up, and before long he was a strong, healthy lad, full of beans. His energy was positively infectious.

Then he developed a passion for the circus — especially the acrobats — which his father, an author of some renown, did not particularly appreciate. In spite of his father's admonishments, Henry regularly left home to join a circus troupe, where he excelled in all sorts of disciplines: trapeze, contortion, juggling, sleight-of-hand. Eventually his father gave in and permitted him to spend several weeks of his summer holiday accompanying the circus on tour. For a little extra pocket money, he always claimed, though his father gave him a generous allowance. The truth of the matter is that my friend was driven by a pathological compulsion to succeed in absolutely everything he tried. This tale of untying knots with his toes was just his style.

Attempting to conceal my amusement, I comforted my sister. 'Next time he will, I'm sure. He was simply trying to overcome his shyness by impressing you with his little trick.'

'You're probably right, but that doesn't make it any less irritating. Listen, James, I want you to talk to him. Discreetly, of course, but you have to make him understand. Or else...'

'Or else what?'

'I shall have to give greater consideration to *John's* proposal,' she answered indifferently. 'True, he doesn't have the best prospects — he's only a mechanic, after all — but he *is* rather charming.'

'What's it to me? I'm not your... Oh!' I cried suddenly. 'Don't do it, Betty. Henry's like a tiger when he's jealous. And you know he'd blame *me*. He's my best friend and I don't want to lose that.'

'Jealous? That's a laugh! He hasn't made the slightest hint of an advance on me! Jealous indeed. What does he have to be jealous of? Anyway, I'm going to...' She broke down in tears. I opted to keep quiet. 'I'm in love with him, James. All this waiting is unbearable. You've got to help me. His parents are in London; he's home alone. Can't you have a word with him?'

'All right,' I said resignedly. 'I'll do my best. But I make no promises. Let's see…' I looked at my watch. 'It's not quite nine o'clock. Henry probably hasn't gone to bed yet.'

Elizabeth walked over to the window and opened the curtains. 'I can't see any lights on over there, but… Oh! James! *James!*' she shrieked.

I leapt to her side.

'I saw a light,' she said with a shudder.

'A light? But there isn't any light. Apart from the street lamp, anyway…'

With a tremulous index finger she indicated the Darnley house. 'I saw a light, I'm positive. Just for a second, but there was a light in the room where Mrs Darnley…'

I looked out across this familiar landscape. We lived on the edge of a small village near Oxford. The road from the left terminated in front of our house. On the other side of that road, a path stretched off into the woods, flanked on either side by a pair of houses. To the right, the White house, and to the left – within the right-angle formed by the road and the path – stood the gloomy, sinister residence of Victor Darnley. The tall red-brick gabled building was largely hidden behind impressive topiaries, and its walls were shrouded in a dark cloak of ivy. A magnificent weeping willow stood in one corner of the garden, and might have brightened the atmosphere were it not for the yews, fir trees, and large conifers behind the house, through which the wind moaned mournfully. The place was grim, and my sister – never overburdened with imagination – had dubbed it 'Wuthering Heights'. The house had acquired its ominous reputation a year or two before the Second World War, when John was about twelve. His father, Victor Darnley, was an industrialist with everything going for him: material prosperity and a happy home life. He was immensely proud of his son, and his wife – a kind, modest woman – was well thought of in the village.

One October evening he returned from London to find the house empty. John's absence was not unusual; he was probably just playing at a friend's house. But Mrs Darnley? She should not have been out at this hour. All searches proved in vain; she had not been seen anywhere. Having located his son, Victor Darnley returned home and searched the entire house from top to bottom. On the uppermost floor – a converted attic – he found a door which appeared to be locked on the inside. In a panic, he forced it open. The spectacle that met his eyes would remain with him for the rest of his days. His wife lay on the floor, drenched in blood. Clutched in her right hand was a kitchen knife, her wrists had been slashed and her body was covered with stab wounds. Since the bolt on the door had been shot, and the window was locked on the inside, the police had no choice but to conclude that it was a suicide. But what a suicide! The unfortunate Mrs Darnley must have suffered a sudden and powerful attack of mania to have killed herself in this manner. There was no conceivable reason for it. Nobody – especially not her husband or son – could come up with a satisfactory explanation.

From that day onwards, Victor descended into a deep melancholy. He grew taciturn and reclusive, only tending to his garden and looking after the house. Before long, his business went bankrupt and he was forced to rent out a few rooms. He kept the ground floor for himself and his son, and leased out the first floor. The first tenants left after only six months, without notice or explanation. After that, war broke out and the army requisitioned the house, so there were a great deal of comings and goings. When peace returned, he rented out the upper floor again, this time to a young couple who were delighted to make the place their home. This, however, did not last. The wife was briefly hospitalised after a nervous breakdown, and simply refused to return to the house. Other couples moved in, but never stayed very long. Their reasons for leaving were always the same: a curious atmosphere of creeping unease, and strange noises in the attic.

This gave the house its sinister reputation, and Victor encountered serious difficulties in finding other tenants. The upper floor remained unoccupied for four months. However, the village was now abuzz with the news that a Mr and Mrs Latimer would soon be moving in.

'It's gone now, but I saw it clearly: it was in the fourth window along. Top floor. The room where Mrs Darnley committed suicide. James. James! What do you make of it?'

'Your mind is playing tricks on you. You know nobody has set foot in that room since…'

'By the way, James, have you heard anything about the couple that are moving in?'

'They're called Mr and Mrs Latimer, that's all I can tell you. Nobody knows anything; if they did, Mother would have found out ages ago.'

Elizabeth shuddered, moving away from the window. 'That house gives me the chills. I wouldn't live there at any price. Poor John; his mother goes mad and kills herself, and now his father's losing his marbles. It's a wonder John himself hasn't gone a little funny, living in that creepy old place.'

'True enough. But he's got nerves of steel, our John. Even in the war, while the bombs were falling, he was never the type to lose his head.'

'Please, James, let's not talk about the war. It's been over for three years now, I can't bear to be reminded of it.'

'That's not my point. All I'm trying to say is that John is a good fellow. A dependable sort who can be relied on, whatever the circumstances.'

'All right, all right. I can quite see what you're driving at. And I *am* fond of him, it's just that…'

'You're in love with Henry. You love him, he loves you; you're both so in love with each other that you're afraid to say so out loud.' I put on my jacket. 'But fear not! Your big brother is here to sort everything out for you.'

She put her hands on my shoulders, fixing me with a look of both gratitude and concern. 'Don't be too obvious about it, James. He might think it was me that told you…'

'But it is!' I laughed. 'Don't worry. I'm not an idiot, I know what I'm doing. You might as well announce the engagement now,' I added on my way out of the door.

2
NIGHTMARE

I took my key, knowing I probably wouldn't be back until late. As I left the house via the front door, I experienced a sudden sense of impending danger. Though I could determine no reason for it, it proved difficult to shake. I scanned my surroundings as I walked. The gathering fog dulled the light from the lone street lamp, and accentuated the disquieting atmosphere of the Darnley residence. I fixed my gaze on its upper floor, watching for the tiniest hint of a light. But the whole place was in darkness.

I pushed open the gate and crossed the road, shaking my head and endeavouring to get my thoughts in order. The simplest solution is often the correct one, I thought. After Mrs Darnley's suicide, her husband had begun to lose his mind and his will to live. Soon afterwards, there came both noises from the attic and mysterious lights in the upper windows. Before Elizabeth told me about it, Henry was the first to broach the subject. He even queried John, who was nonplussed because to his knowledge not a soul had been up there since his mother died.

The explanation? Well, it was childishly simple: under cover of darkness, Victor had been venturing into the haunted room in the hope of catching a glimpse of his late wife's ghost. Poor fellow, I thought. I could picture the scene quite clearly: candle in hand, dressed in his nightshirt and cap, he cautiously climbs the staircase to the attic for a reunion with his lost love. Yes, that had to be it.

Having covered the hundred yards between our home and the Whites', I rapped three times on the front door. Henry answered quickly.

'Excellent timing, James. I was getting rather bored.' Though diminutive in stature, Henry had an above-average physique, which made him look rather stout. His round face, crowned with a mop of thick curly hair parted down the middle, betrayed both kindness and a certain intensity.

We shook hands firmly, then headed through to the drawing room.

'To be honest,' I commenced in what I hoped was a natural-sounding voice, 'I'm at a bit of a loose end myself.'

'What a coincidence,' said Henry with a friendly wink.

I gave him a knowing smile and sank into an armchair, already losing faith in my deception. Henry went over to the drinks cabinet and I heard him moan, 'Oh, the rotter. He's hidden the nicest whisky in his desk.'

The rotter in question was Henry's father. Henry rattled the top drawer of the desk. 'Locked! Can you believe it? Is there no trust left in the world? Still, if he thinks that little lock is going to stop me…'

He seized a paperclip and, with a flick of the wrist, the drawer was open. Very few locks could withstand his dexterous fingers. I recalled his earliest experiments when we were small, on the cupboard where his mother locked away the jam.

'To melancholy autumn evenings,' he said, raising the whisky bottle in triumph.

'And what if your parents come home early? I doubt your father would be too pleased to see you've been pillaging his private reserve.'

'We're doing him a favour, really. He shouldn't drink so much at his age anyway. You pour, I'll fetch the cigars.'

'Singles? Or doubles?' I inquired solemnly.

'Whichever you like.' Meaning, filled to the brim.

Henry slipped out of the room while I played waiter. I picked up a magazine from the table and sank into an armchair. Skimming the pages, I noticed the margins were crammed with pencilled annotations.

'Henry,' I said when my host returned, 'do you always scribble comments on magazine articles?'

'You mean you don't?'

'What?'

'My dear fellow, reading without annotating is like eating without digesting.'

I waited patiently for him to explain. He smiled. 'It's a phrase my father has grown fond of repeating. To be honest, I find it very irritating. I tell you, James, it's not easy being the son of an author! Sometimes he disappears into his study for two or three days at a time, and other times he chatters to us non-stop, all the while making notes about something different altogether. Mother is used to it by now, but it really gets on my nerves. Anyway...'

Arthur White was a distinguished novelist. After completing his medical studies, he had worked as an assistant to a Harley Street physician before establishing his own practice. To pass the time between patients, he started writing short stories. One by one, they appeared in the pages of a popular London weekly, and were met with great success. On the advice of his delighted editor, Arthur White abandoned his medical practice – which was going nowhere anyway – and became a literary celebrity.

Apart from the short stories he penned for the magazine, which had launched his career, he also wrote mysteries, thrillers, science fiction, and some rather successful historical novels. He did all he could to encourage his son to follow in his footsteps, but Henry's interests were the polar opposite of his own.

We sipped our whisky in silence.

'They won't be back for a while yet,' said my friend after a pause. 'Father has taken Mother to London, to the theatre. After that they're heading to a party with some friends. I doubt they'll be home before two in the morning.'

I grinned at him to show I had taken his point: the bottle would be finished long before then. That's when I remembered the reason I had come over in the first place, though I had no idea how to tackle the delicate subject. We talked of this and that until, to my immense relief, Henry put me out of my misery. Without losing his relaxed tone, he lowered his voice. 'James, there's something I'd like to discuss with you. In fact, it's about your sister.'

I feigned surprise in the ensuing silence. Henry took the bottle and gave me a quizzical look. I nodded and he topped up our drinks, then sat back down and studied his glass thoughtfully before downing it in one. He opened his mouth as though to speak, but decided against it. Then he took an unusually long time to light a cigar. He was clearly struggling to conceal his embarrassment, so I took the lead.

'Well, what's she been up to?'

'Nothing. Nothing at all. And that's the problem. The other day I was about to kiss her, but changed my mind at the last moment.'

'Whatever for?'

'I care for her a great deal.'

'Then why didn't you kiss her?'

Sensing that Henry was taken aback by my tone, I spoke a little more gently. 'If you care for her, there's no reason you shouldn't kiss her. When two people are in love with one another – which certainly seems to be the case here – they kiss. It's perfectly natural. Normal. There's no reason not to. Understand, Henry? No reason at all. Since the dawn of time, men and women…' I was getting carried away. More calmly, I said, 'Henry old man, why didn't you kiss her when the urge took you? There's no need to gawp at me like that. Why not, for heaven's sake?'

Henry was frozen, looking stunned. He swallowed a couple of times, then finally said, 'But that's what I'm trying to tell you, James. Listen, are you feeling all right? You know, if you can't handle your whisky, maybe you shouldn't…'

'Me? Not handle my whisky? You must be joking.'

I took the bottle and refilled my glass under Henry's troubled gaze, then gestured for him to continue.

'Well, I was about to kiss her when suddenly…'

I stared expectantly.

'Suddenly… I had doubts.'

'Doubts?'

'Doubts. *Doubts.*'

'All right, I heard you the first time. What sort of doubts?'

He rubbed his forehead and gazed at the floor. 'I wasn't sure that Elizabeth felt the same way, so I managed to play it off.'

Play it off? What a joke. He undid knots with his toes, and to him that was 'playing it off'. I fought back the urge to burst out laughing, and started hiccupping instead. With a swig of whisky, I managed to compose myself.

'Henry,' I sighed. 'All I can tell you is this: Elizabeth *does* have feelings for you. Feelings which run considerably deeper than ordinary friendship.'

I waited a moment for my words to sink in. Henry finally managed to say, 'What you mean is that…'

'What I mean is that she's in love with you.'

'That she's in love with me!' he cried out, overcome with emotion. 'James, you're not just saying that, are you? I mean, you're really sure…'

'Obviously, she hasn't said as much outright,' I lied with somewhat troubling ease, 'she's much too proud for that. But she can't fool me. She has all the symptoms of a young woman very much in love.'

'James,' Henry cut in, 'are you sure it's *me* she's in love with? Couldn't it be John? If you saw the way he's been looking at her lately...' A look of jealousy – the 'green-eyed monster' – flickered in Henry's eyes. I did not like to think what might happen if he were to catch Elizabeth and John in each other's arms.

I held up a hand to placate him. 'No, Henry, it's you. I'm her brother, I know well enough what goes on in her head. Elizabeth in love with John?' I shrugged. 'Certainly not. He's a chum. A pal. No more than that.'

Reassured, Henry raised his glass in a toast to John, in view of the fellow's recent misfortunes. Then he raised a second toast to Elizabeth, the most beautiful girl in England. We were in a kind of euphoria now, and it only grew stronger as the evening wore on. Soon we were completely inebriated.

Sure of himself once more, Henry started to brag of all the glories yet to come. He would be the greatest and strongest acrobat of them all, there was nothing he couldn't do! Frankly, all the 'me, me, me,' business started to get on my nerves. Henry was a decent sort, it's true, but his perpetual desire to be the centre of attention was, to be perfectly honest, insufferable.

Next, he treated me to a variety of circus tricks. He was a gifted acrobat, no doubt about it, but the notion of doing it for a living – let alone becoming a worldwide sensation – was altogether different. Though he was my best friend, I didn't like the idea of my sister marrying an egomaniacal acrobat.

But I soon realised he was just drunk. When I pointed this out to him, he informed me that I wasn't entirely sober either. We looked at each other for a few seconds, then burst into fits of hysterical laughter. I rose on unsteady feet to solemnly toast the royal family. Henry did likewise, before slumping into his chair again. I sat back down, utterly sloshed. Then Henry summoned the strength to drink one last toast to his beloved. I didn't care for the idea of Elizabeth seeing either of us in this wretched state. Whatever would she think of her big brother, who was usually so dignified?

'What are you up to now, old chap?' I murmured. Henry was throwing a little ball into the air.

'Juggling.'

A fresh burst of hilarity, then he explained, 'It's a little trick of mine. I'll show you one of these days.'

'No, you'll show me now,' I insisted.

'It needs a certain set of circumstances, and… and…' with that, he slumped back and fell into a deep sleep.

Out of sympathy, I decided to do likewise. I switched off the lamp and permitted myself to slide into a blissful slumber.

A woman is pushing a pram. The child is moaning – weakly, sometimes scarcely audible at all. But the woman is imperturbable. She continues pushing the pram. The moans become full-throated cries; the child is unhappy, it is suffering, it is consumed by terrible sorrow. It is crying out for help, though nobody seems to hear. There is something strange about the child's face, it is not like a newborn at all, but that of a full-grown adult. An adult whom I happen to recognise.

It is Henry.

I awoke with a start, drenched in sweat, to find myself still in that darkened room. I tried in vain to gather my thoughts, but was thwarted by a crippling headache. It felt as though a carousel was spinning in my poor skull. Suddenly, a groan from somewhere nearby put a stop to that infernal carousel. I listened. Nothing. Was I still trapped in a nightmare? Wide-eyed, I peered into the darkness and managed to make out a few shapes. Where was I? Not in my own bed, that much was certain. I was caught somewhere between dream and reality.

Bit by bit, I returned to my senses. I was suffering one hell of a hangover, and had just begun trying to analyse my dream when a moan in the darkness made me jump. Somewhere in this room, I was sure of it. Henry – it had to be Henry. We were the only ones in that drawing room. Those moans turned to sobs, just as they had in my dream; Henry was weeping. Poor Henry, he was having a nightmare too. He began mumbling in his delirium: 'No… it's too horrible… I don't want to. Mummy, don't leave… I'm begging you…' He woke with a start. 'What's going on? James?'

'I'm here, Henry. Calm down. You were having a nightmare, that's all. Stay where you are, I'll put the light on.'

Groping around in the darkness, I finally managed to turn on the standard lamp without knocking it over. Henry was white as a sheet, with red-rimmed eyes. On his face was a look of profound distress. I went over and put a hand on his shoulder to comfort him.

'As a matter of fact I just had a nightmare myself.' I tried to smile. 'We rather asked for it, don't you think?'

He didn't seem to hear me. 'It was a horrible nightmare. Horrible. But worst of all…'

'Nightmares are seldom pleasant.'

'The worst part is that I can't remember…'

'Then what are you upset about? Don't move, I'll go and make us some coffee. Everything will look better after some coffee, you'll see.'

'James!' he cried, staring at the clock in horror.

'What's wrong?'

'It's nearly half-past three!'

'So what?'

'My parents aren't home yet.'

'But you said yourself they wouldn't be back before three,' I pointed out in a soothing voice.

'You're right,' he conceded, 'plus they have rather a long drive. Honestly, I don't know what's wrong with me…'

'What's wrong with *us*,' I said ironically, indicating the hollow shell of the whisky bottle. With that, I went out to make the coffee.

After three cups, Henry began to emerge from his stupor. 'That's better. But I wish I could remember this nightmare that upset me so much. For the life of me, I don't know...'

The telephone rang, making us both jump. Frozen in his seat, Henry stared at me in horror. Then he finally stood up, walked slowly towards it, and reached out hesitantly for the receiver. With a deep breath, he picked it up.

That feeling of indefinable dread which had crept over me when I left home hours earlier suddenly returned. I lit a cigarette and forced myself to watch the swirls of smoke curling from its tip.

Henry hung up. Seconds passed, and the silence grew unbearable. He stood motionless, his eyes fixed on the phone. Finally, he turned his head towards me. A gaunt, pale face, ravaged by suffering.

'There's been an accident. My mother is dead.'

3

A SINGULAR SUICIDE

Arthur White had lost control of his nippy little convertible while driving home from London at roughly three in the morning. The car had rolled over on top of its occupants. Thanks to his remarkable stamina, Arthur himself emerged unscathed. After he had endured nearly twenty minutes with a ton of twisted metal lying on top of him, a group of passers-by finally succeeded in extricating him from the wreck. He was lucky; most men would have been paralysed for life after a smash like that. Tragically, Mrs White was not so fortunate. She died at approximately half-past three.

Arthur White had first met Louise, the woman who would become his wife, while he was still a practising physician. She was the elder sister of one of his young patients, a terminally ill child. He and Louise took turns to sit a vigil by the little one's bedside, who eventually died a few weeks before their scheduled wedding day. They were married in a private ceremony.

I had seen their wedding photographs. They were an attractive couple indeed: he tall, dark, and handsome; she a petite and graceful blonde with dainty hands and feet. She seemed to radiate warmth and happiness to everyone around her, a beacon of perpetual good cheer. Everyone – particularly children – loved her. I used to make up excuses to visit Henry's house, simply so that I could be near her.

Well, there was also Arthur White's private gymnasium. He

used to train there for an hour a day before heading out for a walk in the country, whatever the weather. As soon as his back was turned, Henry and I used to sneak into the gym and mess around with the equipment. Mrs White was quite happy for us to do it, as long as we made sure everything was put back in its rightful place before her husband returned. She used to reward us with food – I can still taste the muffins slathered with homemade marmalade. I've never had better.

Her violent death came as a real shock to the village, where she was universally admired. Arthur plunged into a deep depression, blaming himself for the accident. As for Henry, he was inconsolable. Nothing and nobody could ease his sorrow. My friend had always been close to his family, particularly his mother, whom he adored above all others. You might think this is perfectly normal, but there was always something a little obsessive in the way Henry worshipped his mother. It made his horror at her death all the more intense. From the moment he heard the dreadful news, he was positively prostrate with grief.

Mrs White's funeral was a difficult, deeply emotional affair. The only one who displayed a semblance of composure was Victor Darnley. His face was etched with sadness, though this was mainly out of compassion for his friends. I can still hear the astonishing words he uttered during the ceremony: 'Don't weep for her, Arthur. Be happy for her. You see, death is not the end. The pain you feel now, I have also felt – and just as badly. It seems as though you've lost her forever. But don't worry. She will be back. You will see her again soon. Believe me, my friend, you will see her again.'

'Poor Henry, we've simply got to help him. We can't just leave him like this. I've tried everything, but he's inconsolable. He won't listen to me. This isn't going to be easy.'

The tall red-headed fellow who spoke these words was John Darnley, a splendidly sympathetic chap who was always out to help those in need.

The three of us — Henry, John, and I — used to meet in the pub on Saturday evenings. That Saturday was no exception, though Henry only stayed a little while, and appeared more taciturn than ever.

It was only just nine o'clock. Sitting in our customary corner, we stared at the empty chair, which our friend had just vacated. We liked this vast low-ceilinged room with its broad beams blackened by generations of cigarette smoke, its oaken panels, its bar, which served the best beer in the county. Behind that bar stood the formidable Fred, a publican par excellence when it came to cultivating a warm, friendly atmosphere. He was filling tankard after tankard with foam and amber liquid, amid general chatter and a sheet of smoke that grew thicker with every hour, dimming the meagre glow of the wall lamps.

But we were in no mood to celebrate. The concern in John's eyes mirrored my own.

'James, do you think Elizabeth might be able to do something? You could ask her, at least.'

The suggestion obviously pained him, but he made it anyway — that's the sort of fellow he was. I knew he was in love with my sister, and yet what he was asking me to do could only push Elizabeth away from him and into Henry's arms.

I shook my head. 'Elizabeth, the wet lettuce? Better not, she'd probably make him worse. She has a knack for upsetting the very people she's trying to comfort.' After a brief pause, I continued with an air of self-assurance, 'Henry will get through this, it's only a matter of time. Time heals all wounds. If not for that, I doubt any of us could endure our sorrows...'

I stopped short, shocked by my own clumsiness.

'Time heals all wounds,' said John thoughtfully. 'I suppose it does. Partially, at least. Let's just say it gives the scars a chance to form.'

I could have kicked myself – how stupid of me! But the damage was already done, and John began recounting his own night of horror. 'I was playing at Billy's house that evening, and Dad came to fetch me. He was frantic, he said Mum had gone missing. We went home, but she wasn't there. Dad headed upstairs… then he gave a cry unlike anything I'd heard before in my life. I bolted up the stairs, to the top floor. The door at the end of the passage – the fourth door – was open, and light was spilling out. I ran forward and saw Mum lying on the floor, with Dad on his knees next to her.'

'I'm sorry, John,' I murmured.

He continued as though he hadn't heard me: 'I was about ten years old then. Dad was never the same afterwards. They say he went mad. And we lost everything. I had to give up my studies and find a job to support us.' He looked down at the rough skin of his hands. 'But that wasn't the worst of it. Mum was dead. She might have died in an accident – these things happen – but to commit suicide… and what a suicide! She went insane in the space of a few hours. Completely mad. You should have seen the state of her body. It looked like the work of some escaped lunatic. But that was impossible – the room was locked on the inside. I've lost count of the number of nights the question has kept me awake: why did she do it? Why? You know, I never fully accepted the idea that she went mad. All the same…' He could scarcely hold back his tears.

What a fool I was. I couldn't even find the words to console him. Silently, I cursed myself. How could I have stirred up all these dreadful memories? All I could think to do was offer him a cigarette. James, what an idiot you are.

'It's not your fault, James. It was bound to happen. Henry lost his mother ten days ago; I lost mine ten years ago. There are two widowers living opposite one another, how could I fail to make the connection?'

This only made me feel worse for having failed to make just such a connection. John gave me a hearty slap on the back, declaring, 'Come now, James! Don't worry about it, it's all in the past. Don't fret about me, it's Henry we should be worrying about now.'

He gave Fred a wave; the publican nodded knowingly. Two frothy tankards of beer appeared on the table almost immediately. 'This round is on me, gentlemen,' Fred boomed with a broad grin.

He always spoke so stridently, and with dramatic gestures, so there could be no doubt who ran the place, no matter how loud the surrounding chatter might be. His expression turned grave, and he placed a hand on each of our shoulders before speaking with sudden urgency. 'You've got to snap him out of it. Henry, I mean. You can't let him shut himself away. He's had a bit of bad luck, the poor fellow, but…'

He was interrupted by shouts from the bar: more customers.

'Anyway, I'll leave you to it. Yes, yes, I'm coming!' he roared.

'The Latimers moved in last night,' John said after a short pause.

The shock of Mrs White's death had caused me to forget about the arrival of the new tenants. I had caught only the briefest glimpse of them that afternoon. 'What are they like?'

'He's in his forties. Blond hair. An insurance salesman apparently. She's quite a beauty: long dark hair and a perfect smile. About thirty-five, I'd say. A shame she's married,' he added with a wink.

'Are they friendly?'

'As far as I can tell, though we haven't had much chance to chat. Polite, anyway.'

'And they haven't mentioned anything about…'

'Footsteps at night? Mysterious lights in the attic? And all the other products of fertile imaginations?'

'Well, John, you ought to know by now! Plenty of other tenants have encountered them, haven't they? What's more, none of them have stayed very long, have they?'

'I'm quite aware our house has a rather disturbing atmosphere. A woman went mad and killed herself there in truly horrible circumstances, after all. And Father hasn't been himself for a long time; sometimes his behaviour can be a little strange… but he's not mad, no matter what people might think. These two facts cause people's imaginations to work overtime, that's all. A creaky staircase? Nothing unusual about that, is there? Last time I checked, it was made out of wood! And they only hear it at night? Well, everyone else is asleep – the house is silent, that's why! As for the footsteps in the attic and the mysterious lights… I can tell you for a fact that I've never encountered anything like that.'

'You sleep on the ground floor,' I remarked. 'So you wouldn't hear or see anything going on in the attic.'

'True enough,' he said, 'but nobody goes up there. Let's assume these gossips are telling the truth – who could it be? Who would have the absurd idea of playing at ghosts? I just can't see it myself.'

I held my tongue. There was no point advancing my own theory, which seemed to be the only plausible explanation: that his father believed Mrs Darnley was going to come back to him one day; that he was searching for her under cover of darkness, in the very place where she had left him. There was also the matter of Victor's remarks to Arthur at Louise's funeral: 'She will be back. You will see her again soon.' Not much room for doubt, though I couldn't bring myself to try and explain this to John. If there was one subject that was bound to upset him even further, it was the prospect of his father's descent into madness.

Better to keep quiet. I had put my foot in it quite enough for one day.

John didn't say a word. His mind was obviously elsewhere.

Suddenly, he spoke. 'Last night I helped the Latimers move in.'

I took a cigarette from the pack on the table. John hesitated again, then continued, 'Mrs Latimer was chatting to my father.'

I calmly lit the cigarette.

'Mr Latimer and I were carrying the suitcases.'

I took a drag and exhaled smoke towards the ceiling.

'While we did that, Father and Mrs Latimer waited in the hall.'

I drummed the table with my fingertips.

'We carried the cases up to the first floor…'

I sighed.

'And then we headed back downstairs. That's when…'

'That's when what?' I asked, trying to keep my voice calm.

'That's when I heard a snippet of their conversation. The conversation between Father and Mrs Latimer, that is.'

Losing patience, I rapped the table with my knuckles. 'And? What were they saying?'

'I didn't hear the beginning, but I reckon Father was telling her why the previous tenants left in such a hurry. You know, the footsteps and all the rest. But Mrs Latimer's reply… well, it was rather strange. I don't know what to make of it.'

I cleared my throat. 'And what did she say?'

'She said: "I'm not afraid of ghosts. Quite the opposite, in fact."'

'Quite the opposite?'

'Those were her exact words: "Quite the opposite." She didn't say anything after that; just a quick good-night to Father before heading up to her room.'

'So she's a ghost-fancier.'

'I beg your pardon?'

'She's not afraid of ghosts, she *likes* them.'

'But that's bizarre. Nobody likes ghosts, do they?'

'I can think of things plenty more bizarre than that,' I said with a sigh. I was thinking of that night I had spent at Henry's ten days earlier. When he woke with a start from a dreadful nightmare, seized by inexplicable sorrow. The words he had murmured in his sleep: 'No… it's too horrible… I don't want to. Mummy, don't leave… I'm begging you…' This was at half-past three – the very moment she died!

'Are you talking about the Whites' car accident?' John asked, frowning.

'Yes. Well, no,' I stammered. 'No, it's nothing. I don't know what I'm talking about. I'm just tired, that's all.'

When John suggested we call it a night, I didn't object.

4

A LETTER TO LOUISE

'Darling, I've got a terrible headache.'
'Try some aspirin, dear.'
'I've already had four, it's no use.'
'You have to give them time to work,' replied Father, straightening his tie. 'Come along now, we're running late.'
'Such an awful migraine,' Mother moaned, 'it's excruciating. I can't go out like this. It's just not possible.'
'What?' Father snapped. 'Can't go? When Mr White has shown such courage in overcoming his grief, and organised a lunch out of the goodness of his heart for us to meet the Latimers? You don't want to go because of a little headache? Very poor form, my dear. Come now, chin up.'
Mother stiffened, turning pale, and answered frostily, 'I don't feel well enough to go, so I'm not going.'
Silence.
Father looked as though he might explode, but managed to maintain his composure and placid expression. 'Darling,' he said, taking her by the hand and inclining his head, 'there's nothing worse than a pesky migraine, I know that as well as anybody. I suffer with them myself all too often – particularly at night. But I don't like to bother you, so do you know what I do? I suffer in silence. A migraine is unpleasant, but it's no reason to leave Arthur in the lurch. He needs to be surrounded by friendly faces; it's barely three weeks since he lost his wife! He's utterly

distraught, and Henry's no use. Quite the opposite, in fact. This invitation is a cry for help! He'd never forgive us if we didn't turn up.'

He was met with an icy glare.

'Is that it?'

'What?'

'Have you finished your little tirade?'

'I beg your pardon?' said Father, feigning incomprehension.

'I've had enough of this. We're not going, and that's the end of it. James and Elizabeth can explain. Arthur will understand completely.'

'"We"?' echoed Father, losing his self-control. 'What do you mean, "we"?'

'You and I, that's what I mean. Don't play the fool, you've never been very good at it.'

Father answered grandiosely, 'Your lack of manners and decorum is no concern of mine. You may remain here, madam, but rest assured that *I* will not. Come, children.'

Mother's voice quivered with (feigned) indignation and (genuine) fury. 'You'd leave a sick woman all alone, to be preyed on by some maniac? Don't you read the newspapers?' Then, her eyes aglow with rage, she gave an imperious gesture. 'Very well. Go.'

Father walked in a dignified manner towards the door, then slowed, finally stopped and went to the drinks cabinet. He poured himself a stiff whisky, which he downed in one, before saying softly, 'Off you go, children.'

Once again, Mother had triumphed.

'Don't forget the key,' Elizabeth reminded me as I closed the front door.

'Yes, yes,' I mumbled. 'Dear me, it's humid.'

The day had been particularly hot for late September. A harsh winter was forecast, but for now the south of England was in the midst of a heatwave.

'We might have a storm tonight,' said my sister, examining her outfit with a critical eye. 'How do I look, James?'

'All right,' I said. In fact, she was ravishing in her white sundress, which accentuated her slim figure. The picture was completed by dainty flat-heeled pumps, a lace shawl to conceal a modest neckline and a deceptively simple hairstyle.

'Not bad, not bad at all,' I said. 'Wait a moment. Here, just give your lipstick a dab with this handkerchief. There — that's much better.'

'Do you think Henry will like it?'

'How should I know? Anyway, how are you two getting on these days?'

'Fine, but I think I might have upset him a bit the other day.'

'Oh?'

'Maybe I should have just let him kiss me…'

I waited for her to continue.

'I went over to his house the night before last to check in on him. You know, to see if he was feeling any better,' she went on. 'He was talking about his mother again. About how much she meant to him. We talked about love. Love in all its forms, I suppose. He was very sad, so I tried to comfort him. Then he took me in his arms…'

Not before time, I thought.

'And he kissed me.'

At last! Now we could finally move on with our lives.

'Well, he *tried* to kiss me, but naturally I didn't let him. Not like that, not for the very first time. What's the matter, James?'

My head was in my hands. I could scarcely believe what I was hearing. 'Elizabeth, for God's sake…'

'He wasn't upset or anything like that. He apologised immediately. But there's one thing that bothers me — he said,

"It won't happen again, Elizabeth." I hope he didn't misread the signs. What do you reckon, James?'

By then we had reached the Whites' house, so I didn't answer her. I was fed up with the whole business, and determined not to involve myself in it ever again.

Arthur White answered the door. In spite of his grief, he was perfectly affable. 'Come in, children. How beautiful you look, Elizabeth! That dress suits you wonderfully.'

'Thank you, Mr White,' Elizabeth simpered, blushing with delight.

'But where are your parents?'

'I'm afraid Mother has a terrible migraine and…'

'Your father preferred not to leave her alone. I understand completely, one can't be too careful…' his voice wavered slightly. 'Go on through to the drawing room, John and Henry are waiting for you there.'

As soon as we entered the room in question, two pairs of eyes fixed themselves eagerly on Elizabeth. She ignored them and went to greet Victor Darnley first of all. Since Louise White's death, Victor Darnley seemed to have come out of his shell a little. He had visited Arthur several times, something he'd never really done previously. He complimented Elizabeth in gallant fashion – particularly for such a reticent fellow. She positively purred with pleasure, her coquetry belied by the sparkle in her eyes. To conceal his embarrassment, John joined in with his father's flattery in a somewhat forced manner. As for Henry, flummoxed by the breathtaking sight of Elizabeth blossoming like a sunflower amid all these compliments, the only words he could muster were 'Good evening, Elizabeth.'

'What are you waiting for, Henry?' boomed Arthur White. 'See to our guests!'

The doorbell rang again. 'Ah! The guests of honour. Excuse me,' said Arthur, disappearing into the hall.

It was Victor Darnley who made the introductions. I liked Patrick Latimer immediately, but a vague, indefinable instinct warned me to be careful. It was, however, his wife Alice who was the centre of attention. She was beautiful and knew it, elegantly dressed, albeit a little too provocatively for my taste.

Henry was captivated, positively devouring her with his eyes as she sat down beside him. This did not escape my sister, who turned white with rage when she noticed how awestruck he was. To conceal his discomfiture, Henry went through his usual roster of magic tricks, outdoing himself with each remarkable sleight-of-hand. He put on quite a show, and Patrick Latimer was duly impressed. As for Alice, she gushed with praise, nearly swooning with admiration for what she called Henry's 'powers'. This encouraged him further. His pleasure and pride at being the focal point of the party was obvious, and he moved on to a few more ambitious illusions.

'Henry seems to have regained some of his *joie de vivre*,' I whispered slyly in my sister's ear.

'Shut up,' she hissed.

Arthur somewhat irritably brought an end to his son's performance by asking him to fetch the *hors d'oeuvres* while he opened the champagne. It was a high-quality brut; our host had excelled himself in his generosity.

The champagne sparkled in the glass flutes. It was going to be a pleasant evening after all. Everyone began to relax – even Arthur. Elizabeth was the only one who struggled to hide her jealousy.

'I've read most of your books, Mr White. How do you come up with such clever plots?'

'My inspiration comes from reading, my dear. As I always say, reading without making notes is like eating without digesting.'

'How original! I'll try to remember that...'

Even Victor was more loquacious than usual. 'Arthur is an author for the ages, there's no doubt about it.'

'Well, let's not exaggerate...'

'Excellent champagne, Arthur. I think I'll have a drop more.'

'Help yourself, Victor! My home is your home, as you know.'

'Oh, Henry! How extraordinary! However did you do it?'

'Well, you see, madam—'

'Please call me Alice.'

'Well, *Alice*, it's a gift. I've had it since I was a child.'

'How wonderful!'

'That woman's getting on my nerves, with her flattery and that low-cut dress. Do you think Mrs Latimer is beautiful, John?'

'She's all right, I suppose, if you like that sort of thing. But she's not my type. She can't hold a candle to you, Elizabeth. I swear you've never looked lovelier.'

'Don't make fun of me, John.'

'Heaven forbid, Elizabeth! Look at me, do I look as though I'm lying? Can't you see in my eyes what it is that I'm dying to say to you...?'

'Oh, John...'

The evening was a roaring success by the time the storm broke. It made Alice jump. 'I had a feeling this might happen, it's been so hot today. I don't like it. I can't stand thunderstorms.'

There came a second flash of lightning, accompanied by a resounding clap of thunder. Alice was shaking, and her husband rushed over to comfort her. 'Darling, why don't you have a lie-down if you're feeling unwell? Would that be all right with you, Mr White?'

'Certainly. But may I ask what's the matter? I was a doctor for many years, though I'm no longer practising. If there's anything I can do to assist…'

Alice did not reply. Her gaze was curiously fixed, and her limbs were trembling as her husband helped her over to the sofa. Her breathing was heavy and erratic, so the silk of her bodice looked as though it might tear.

The storm grew more intense and it started to rain. Through the French window overlooking the moor it was possible to see the ink-black sky spliced by copious lightning flashes, each one following the last at such speed that it may as well have been broad daylight. It was a spectacle of terrifying primal beauty, accompanied by an apocalyptic din.

Nobody said a word. The storm was certainly troubling, but not as much as the state Alice was in. She seemed almost catatonic.

'Don't worry,' her husband announced. 'She's a medium. I think she may be slipping into a trance. Perhaps we could dim the lights…'

'I'll turn off the chandelier,' said Henry, his voice uneasy. 'We can switch on the little lamp by the window.'

'No,' Patrick protested. 'The light will be in her eyes. It would be better to use the standard lamp over there, beside the bookcase.'

Henry complied. The room was now plunged into semi-darkness, and the assembled company formed a circle around the sofa. Alice's chest continued heaving, she began to groan and her eyelids half-opened.

Patrick raised his hand for silence. We held our breath.

The medium's lips parted, and she began to utter strange words. 'The land of mists… all I see are shadows and fog. A land where nothing is as it seems, because nothing is real… These creatures are not alive, they are just prisoners trapped in time…' Her voice trailed off.

'Darling,' her husband asked softly, 'can you see anything else?'

After a moment she murmured, 'No, the mists are fading, the shadows are receding, everything is getting dark. Wait a moment... Yes... There are two women. They are arguing; one is trying to come forward but the other is holding her back... I can see the first woman clearly now... Her whole body is covered in terrible wounds... Her wrists... She is pointing her finger accusingly... She is pointing at *me*... No, I can't bear it! Her face is terrifying!'

'It's Eleanor,' Victor said in a whisper. 'It's my wife. She's trying to tell us something.'

Turning deathly pale, he advanced towards Alice. 'Mrs Latimer, it's my wife Eleanor. I'm sure of it. I have... I have received *messages* as well. She's trying to tell me something. Please try, I beg of you.'

Alice closed her eyes. 'Mrs Latimer, I beg of you.'

'It's better not to force it,' said Patrick. 'It might be dangerous...'

Suddenly Alice resumed, louder this time, 'The woman has gone, but her companion is still there. She looks unsure. She doesn't know which way to go. She wants someone to talk to her. No, not *someone*. She wants *one* person to talk to her. A specific person. One person in this very room... Somebody tall and strong, who has travelled part of this road with her...'

All eyes were on Arthur, who looked petrified.

'She wishes... to speak with him *alone*...'

Silence.

'It's you, Mr White. It has to be,' Patrick declared, looking thoughtfully at his wife. 'As for the woman who wants to speak with you... your wife, I presume.'

A blinding flash of lightning illuminated the drawing room, showing the disbelief etched on Arthur's face. Patrick waited for the thunder to cease before continuing, 'I don't wish to fill you with false hope, Mr White, but there may be a way to... Well, it's an experiment we've tried in the past and... I think my wife may be particularly receptive this evening.'

Victor Darnley grabbed his friend's arm. 'Arthur, we have to try!'

Arthur bowed his head in assent.

'This experiment is tough to pull off,' said Patrick, extracting a handkerchief from his breast pocket and dabbing his brow. 'In fact, it's only worked once, and that was several years ago; we had only just married. You must ask your wife a question, Mr White. A question that only she would be able to answer. But don't ask it in words – write it on a piece of paper, and keep it out of sight. You will then place the paper in an envelope, which you will seal, and write your signature across the flap. Or, if you prefer, you could use a wax seal. My wife will need to feel the envelope for a moment or two, and then... and then we'll see what happens. I must reiterate, there is only a very limited chance of success. But you need to decide quickly; my wife could emerge from the trance at any moment.'

Arthur rose abruptly and left the room.

Patrick held up his hands. 'Please, my friends, you must remain silent. Even a single word could have serious consequences.'

Arthur was gone for ten interminable minutes.

'Here,' he said, handing an envelope to Patrick, who in turn showed it to the others. The tip of the flap was sealed with wax, and there were signatures down each oblique side.

Henry whispered to me, 'Father collects rare coins. He must have used one for the stamp.'

Patrick leaned over his wife and placed the envelope in her hands. 'My dear, we have a message. A message for the woman.'

Alice's fingers tightened around the envelope, then slackened. Her husband retrieved it from her and placed it on the coffee table. 'Now,' he said, approaching the window and pointing out,

'I think we might need to wait until the storm passes...'

The end of his sentence was cut off by a blinding flash and a dreadful rumble of thunder. The drawing room was plunged into total darkness.

'Henry,' Arthur said imperiously, 'go and check the fuses.'

'On my way, Father.'

'Everybody else stay where you are,' our host continued. 'Let's not forget, Mrs Latimer is in a trance. The slightest shock could do untold harm to her.'

After a minute, the standard lamp came back on and Henry reappeared. As instructed, nobody else had moved.

'Just the fuses,' Henry explained. 'Has Alice... I mean, has Mrs Latimer said anything?'

'No,' Patrick answered, staring at his shoes. 'But that doesn't mean anything. We must wait.'

Victor was distracted by the envelope on the coffee table. He turned to his friend. 'Anything is possible, Arthur. You mustn't lose faith. I have a feeling...'

A distant flash lit up the sky, and once again the drawing room was in darkness. The silence was palpable.

Henry was the first to break it. 'I'll take care of it, Father. I know the way with my eyes closed.'

'Fetch some candles too, Henry. In fact, fetch the candelabra from the hall, in case we have another blackout. I worry all these disturbances will upset Mrs Latimer. What do you think?'

Patrick Latimer cleared his throat before answering, 'I'm afraid so. The darkness makes it easier to concentrate, but all these upheavals certainly won't help.' He cleared his throat again. '*Ahem*. We mustn't delude ourselves; this experiment is very rarely successful. And yet my wife seemed particularly well-disposed this evening. But I'm afraid these power cuts...'

'I must confess, Mr Latimer, that in spite of my scepticism I had allowed myself a little sliver of hope. But let's be honest, shall we? It's not possible to speak with the dead. All my life, I…'

'Arthur,' Victor cut in sharply, 'you don't know what you're talking about.'

The light came back on. Alice was still on the sofa, and looked to be asleep. In fact, she seemed to be in a slumber so deep that nothing the others might say could disturb her.

'I'm sorry, Mr White. I'm afraid it's impossible,' said Patrick regretfully. 'I think she'll wake now.' He approached his wife and stroked her forehead gently, murmuring into her ear.

'To think I let myself believe…' Arthur said, nodding sadly. 'Anyway, the storm seems to have passed.'

At that moment, Henry burst into the room brandishing a lit candelabra. 'There, now we're prepared for every eventuality… Oh! Alice is…'

All eyes turned towards Alice. She had emerged from her trance at last, and was rearranging her hair. She spoke rather dreamily. 'My God, where am I? Patrick?'

Her husband took her by the hands. 'It's all right, darling, it's over now. You just fainted.'

'Oh, God!' She buried her face in her hands. 'I've ruined this wonderful party! I should have seen it coming when the storm started… Patrick, why didn't you warn me? I do apologise, Mr White…'

'Not your fault, dear lady. There's no need to apologise.'

'Don't you remember anything at all, darling?' asked Patrick, helping her to her feet.

'Why, did I say something?' Alice said, her eyes widening in surprise.

'A few words. Rather vague. You'd better get some rest now. Please excuse us, Mr White, but… Careful, darling!'

Alice had wandered over to the window and was staggering slightly. She clung to an armchair for support. Her husband rushed over to help her, and they both collapsed into the chair, but not before knocking over a small table beside it. Both a table lamp and a potted plant were broken in the confusion.

Agitated discussion ensued, but both parties stuck to their guns: Patrick was determined to pay for the damage, while Arthur wouldn't hear of it. Finally they reached a compromise – the Latimers would invite Arthur over for dinner to make up for it.

Alice's gaze alighted fleetingly on the envelope. It lay right where they had left it, in the centre of the coffee table, forgotten by everyone. Arthur retrieved it discreetly and slipped it into the inside pocket of his jacket.

Observing this, Alice's eyes glazed over, and she spoke in a curiously atonal voice. 'Why, of course he will. Henry will become wise and sensible.'

These words were met with a silence that lasted a few seconds; the others were speechless. Patrick returned to his wife's side; she looked as though she might faint again. She collapsed into his arms and said woefully, 'Darling, I don't know what's happening to me, I'm talking nonsense…'

Suddenly John and Elizabeth – who had not spoken in a long time – dashed over to Arthur's side just in time to catch him; he had collapsed in a dead faint. They installed him in the armchair and slapped him gently to try and revive him. Henry raised a glass of cognac to his father's lips, which finally brought him to his senses.

'Father, what on earth's the matter? Too much champagne?'

Arthur shook his head and pushed his son away. Beads of sweat coursed down his face as he wordlessly removed the envelope from his inside pocket and examined it carefully. He even held it up to the light. Then he beckoned Henry over and gestured for *him* to examine it too.

'Arthur,' Victor said, aghast, 'you don't mean that—'

'This envelope has not been opened,' interrupted Henry. 'I can assure you of that, Father.'

Arthur went over to his desk and rummaged among his papers, returning with a letter opener. In deathly silence, he slipped the blade beneath the flap of the envelope and slit it. He withdrew the sheet of notepaper, unfolded it and showed it to the others.

Written on it was a single sentence:

My dear – is Henry ever going to pull himself together?

5

A VISIT FROM THE DEAD

It was now late October, a month since that extraordinary evening when Mrs White's spirit made its unprecedented appearance.

Naturally, I assumed it to be some trick perpetrated by the Latimers – how else to explain such a remarkable phenomenon? Consider the facts: completely hidden from prying eyes, Arthur White had written on a sheet of notepaper, *My dear – is Henry ever going to pull himself together?* Then he slipped the paper into an envelope, which he subsequently sealed. Apart from a couple of blackouts, the envelope had been in plain sight in the centre of the coffee table the entire time. And then… the impossible occurred. Mrs White gave her reply: 'Why, of course he will. Henry will become wise and sensible.'

Except she didn't. It was *Alice* who spoke, who conveyed this message from beyond. The envelope underwent numerous examinations: the flap had not been peeled or cut in any way; the signatures and the wax seal were intact.

Could Alice have guessed Arthur's question? Or was her answer simply selected at random? Surely this was impossible – it was too precise. Then what?

I could not help but compare this incident to Henry's nightmare. At the very moment of his mother's death, he had awoken in a state of inexplicable sorrow. Not to mention the strange words he uttered in his sleep. It was beyond my comprehension.

Additionally, the subsequent weeks had seen all kinds of rumours about the Darnley house circulating in the village: lights in the haunted room, and the Latimers were frequently troubled by the sound of footsteps overhead.

Fortunately, I had other matters to occupy my mind: my first year of higher education at Oxford, where I was working towards a Bachelor of Arts degree. Henry was in his last year of secondary education, having to repeat the exams he had failed the previous year. He had only himself to blame; he skipped far too many classes. Indeed, he looked set to fail a second time.

Yes, life had certainly been rough for him lately. Was it his mother's death? Naturally, this had affected him greatly. Was it to do with Elizabeth? I don't believe so. He seemed completely detached, as though something altogether different was troubling him.

He argued with his father regularly – almost daily, in fact. Nobody really knew why. My parents asked me about it, no doubt thinking I must be in on the secret. Their shouting matches were so loud you could hear them from our house. I tried talking to him – to help him – but he was evasive. Sometimes, though, his demeanour was oddly upbeat; a stark contrast to his usual edginess and sour mood. Because he *was* on edge; very nervous indeed. Something was bothering him, gnawing at him, but what was it?

I was musing on this question when my eye was caught by the French homework assignment on the desk in front of me. It was peppered with red ink marks. I pushed it to one side in annoyance, cursing the damnable subtleties of French grammar.

Then I looked at my watch: eight o'clock. It was Saturday evening, and Fred would be hurt if I didn't show my face at the pub. I decided to fetch Henry en route.

As I approached the Whites' house, I heard the sound of raised voices: Arthur and Henry were in the midst of another violent quarrel. I froze, unsure how best to proceed, when the front door was hurled open and Arthur came barrelling out, slamming it behind him.

'Good evening, Mr White,' I ventured.

'James!' he cried, looking surprised, then embarrassed. 'Good evening, James, good evening,' he added in a more subdued voice, before rushing off towards the Darnley house. I watched him go. For a month now he had been visiting Victor Darnley every single evening. Their friendship had blossomed quickly – before that, it had been nothing more than mere neighbourliness. I suppose this was understandable, as they had both suffered similar misfortunes. All the same, I couldn't help but feel as though there were something curious about it. I would have to mention it to John.

The light was on in Henry's room. I walked along the path beside the house and peeked inside. Henry was pacing the room agitatedly, his hands behind his back and his head hung low. All at once, he stopped. Evidently he had just had an idea. The furrow in his brow vanished. He opened a drawer in his desk and produced two rubber balls, balancing one on the doorknob and slipping the other into his pocket. What was he up to?

He went into a corner of the room, produced the second ball from his pocket and began throwing it up in the air. Then he hurled it at the floor with all his might; it bounced off the wall, hit the ceiling, then landed… right on top of the other ball.

Bravo, Henry! Another dazzling feat.

I knocked on the window to let him know I was there, then applauded.

He looked surprised, but smiled at me anyway. I showed him my watch and raised an imaginary beer glass to my lips.

*

Fred told one of his jokes as he placed a pair of pints in front of us. I burst out laughing, though I had not found it particularly funny. All Henry could muster was a faint smile. Fred headed back to the bar, still holding his sides, and I lapsed into silence.

Looking Henry firmly in the eye, I asked, 'What's going on, Henry?'

No reply.

'Why all these quarrels with your father?' I persisted, knowing full well that I was being very indiscreet. His silence was getting on my nerves. 'Is it because you've been skipping class again?'

'No. Well, yes, I suppose it's that too. But it's not the main reason.' His eyes gleamed. 'It's about… money.'

'Money? But your father…'

With one hand he covered his eyes; the other he raised to put a stop to this line of questioning. 'James,' he said pleadingly, 'I can't explain it to you. You wouldn't understand. Please, let's talk about something else…'

'Elizabeth?'

He clenched his fists on the table; my question had struck a nerve. 'She rejected me,' he spat. 'She shouldn't have done that.'

Ever since that notorious party his father had hosted in honour of the Latimers, Henry and Elizabeth had been giving each other the cold shoulder. My sister had even let John take her out to dinner one evening, but Henry showed no outward sign of his anger. His pride outweighed his jealousy.

'No, she shouldn't have done that,' he repeated, 'because—'

'Evening, all,' a familiar voice interrupted.

'Hello, John,' said Henry wearily, gesturing to Fred for another round.

John wasn't himself either, and slumped onto the bench.

'Rough day?' said Henry, examining his fingernails.

'Rough night is more like it,' John said, running his hand nervously through his hair. 'Last night, I mean.'

I frowned.

'Hasn't anybody told you?' John asked in surprise.

Silence.

'Frankly,' he continued, 'I don't understand any of it…'

'Here you are, gents,' Fred declared, placing three more beers on the table. Noticing our expressions, his smile faded. He left with a sigh and a shake of the head.

'John,' I implored, 'I need you to do something for me.'

'What's that?'

'If you've got something to tell us, tell us — but do it in one go. None of these long, pregnant pauses, I beg you.'

John didn't seem to hear me. He stared into his beer glass, then took a cigarette from his pocket (without offering one to us) and lit it. 'You already know about the footsteps,' he began. 'I never believed it, myself. But these last few days… I have to confess that I've heard something. And it made me wonder about those tenants who left because they couldn't get a decent night's sleep. It didn't take me long to come up with an explanation: Father's been going up to the attic at night for some reason. Maybe he was trying to see Mother's spirit, or something like that. It doesn't really matter. But that would explain the light in the window as well.'

'I had thought the same thing myself,' I admitted, 'but I was a little worried about mentioning it to you.'

'Well, here's the problem: Father can't be in two places at once.'

I shuddered. Henry remained impassive; his face did not move a single muscle.

'It was nearly nine o'clock,' John continued with that same absent expression. 'We were having coffee with the Latimers, in their drawing room, directly below the attic…' He turned to Henry, suddenly perplexed. 'Your father didn't mention this to you?'

'Not exactly,' Henry answered, looking uncomfortable. 'This morning he said that something strange had happened, but nothing more than that.'

John continued to study him thoughtfully for a moment, then went on, 'Well, we were having coffee, the Latimers, Mr White, my father, and I. By coincidence, we happened to mention the footsteps when all of a sudden we heard them – somebody was walking up and down directly overhead! Back and forth, back and forth, very slowly… they were cautious steps, and not always very clear, but there could be no doubt about it. Someone was pacing in the room above. And Father was by my side the entire time! So much for my little theory.

'Anyway, we all looked at one another, feeling very uneasy. Father turned pale and started trembling. Alice and her husband clung onto one another. The coffee cup fell from Mr White's hand and shattered on the floor. I was the first to regain my composure, so I rushed out into the hall and up the stairs. I kept quiet, though; I didn't want to let the intruder know I was there.

'When I reached the top of the staircase I could still hear the footsteps, but not for long – they stopped almost immediately. But I worked out where they were coming from – it was behind the door on the left. I'd better explain what that hallway looks like: when you get to the top of the stairs, there are only two ways to go. The door on the right opens onto the attic itself. The door on the left opens onto a corridor leading towards a heavy curtain; behind that curtain is a bookcase stuffed with magazines, periodicals, and old newspapers. There aren't any windows on that corridor. In fact, there isn't anything at all except four identical doors down the right-hand side. Like the walls and the ceiling, those doors are panelled with very old, very dark oak. There's no electricity either, so it's pitch-black up there.

'I wasn't foolish enough to head down that corridor alone. I waited for the others, with my ear pressed to the door. Somebody fetched a flashlight. Mr White stayed in the corridor, while Patrick and Father remained at the top of the stairs. Alice and I searched each of the four rooms along that corridor. It was easy enough; the last three were completely empty. The first one had a few bits of old furniture piled up, but nothing more than that. There was nobody in any of those rooms. Each one has a window, but they were all locked on the inside. Of course, I checked behind the curtain at the end of the corridor – all I found were those stacks of old newspapers. No secret passages or anything like that, I know the house well enough to rule that out. But we checked the walls anyway: nothing.'

John breathed a long, heavy sigh. 'I don't understand it. I don't understand anything any more.'

6

A FRENZIED ATTACK

The Darnley house was haunted.

That was the consensus in the village, anyway. This rumour had even reached as far as the capital; a London journalist came out to investigate. The Latimers received frequent evening visitors; there was Arthur, of course, but then there were others, generally of a certain age and financially well off, who were fascinated by the paranormal. The 'ghost' came back twice; of course, Victor was quite convinced it was his wife returning to him.

John soon lost interest in the mystery, focusing all his attention on my sister instead. Although Elizabeth never said as much, I could tell she was developing a certain affection for him.

As for Henry, what is there to be said about him? He seemed edgier and more anxious than ever, with the look of a hunted animal – he who was usually so composed, so confident! His relationship with his father had turned poisonous; their increasingly heated altercations were a constant concern.

In fact, I almost intervened one evening, fearing they might actually come to blows. The tension between them worsened with each passing day.

I was on the point of solving a particularly tricky mathematics problem when Elizabeth came into my room. 'Father's furious!' she cried. 'You'd better come down, have a drink with him. It'll calm him down.'

'What's Mother done now?'

'She won't let him go to the football match tomorrow. It's an important one, apparently. Unfortunately for him, Mother's got her heart set on him taking her to tea…'

'Well, dear sister, why don't *you* go and comfort the pater yourself?'

'Me?' she said, blushing lobster-red. 'Well, I…'

'All right, all right. I get the picture. John's coming to pick you up, and you've only got a few minutes to get ready. Am I right? Go on, get out.'

'You beast,' she yelled as she slammed the door.

The solution to my mathematics problem had disappeared as abruptly as my sister. I went downstairs and found Father in the lounge. 'James, old man!' he called out as soon as I crossed the threshold. He looked to have regained most of his composure, though his hands were still shaking. 'It's the last Saturday in November. Why don't we have a drink? Something a little stronger than tea, eh?'

'That's a rather weak excuse,' I observed sardonically.

'So what? One must drink the wine while it's… While the vines are…' he was searching in vain for a suitable quotation. 'Anyway. Never mind.'

Eyes agleam, he poured two cognacs and we clinked glasses. 'There. That's better,' he sighed, sitting back in his armchair and crossing one leg over the other. 'Women don't think about things the way we do,' he observed. 'They reason with their gut.'

'Father,' I said, feigning astonishment, 'don't let Mother hear you talking like that…'

'Why the hell not? She's the one I'm talking about! She's the *only* one I'm talking about…'

The door opened a crack and Mother appeared. Father froze in his chair.

'Edward,' she said imperiously, 'I've pressed your pearl-grey suit for tomorrow... Oh, how *marvellous*. You're getting our son drunk on whisky.'

'But darling, it's cognac. *French* cognac, no less.'

The door slammed.

Father winced, but swiftly composed himself. 'As I was saying, women reason with... In fact, women don't reason at all! Case in point: tomorrow there's a cup game with Billy Speed playing – the best right-winger in England! Fast, agile, perfect accuracy... In short, it'll be a once-in-a-lifetime match, even for someone who knows *nothing* about football.' He paused. 'Guess what your mother has decided. Any ideas? No? Well, I'll tell you: tea at Wilson's! Can you imagine? With *Billy Speed* playing only a mile away? Incredible! She never ceases to amaze me...' He cleared his throat. 'Anyway, that's not the point I'm trying to make. It's not just your mother's stupidity, it's women in general.' He cited a few other examples which, in his view, supported his argument. It was an in-depth analysis of feminine stupidity from the dawn of time to the present day, concluding with a roster of the hypothetical delights of a world without women.

He didn't believe a word of this drivel; it was just his way of calming himself down, so I listened without interruption.

It was nearly midnight before he finished, and I finally managed to extricate myself. 'I have a mathematics problem to complete, Father.'

'Of course, of course. No rest for the wicked, eh?' He got to his feet and stretched. 'As for me, I'm going to get a breath of fresh air. That cognac was excellent, but my head is a little fuzzy.'

He put on his coat and hat, lit a cigarette, and left the room.

That mathematics problem can wait, I thought, pouring myself the last drop of cognac. Glass in hand, I went over to the fireplace, letting the warmth of both the embers and the alcohol course through me. I heard somebody come into the lounge behind me.

'James,' said my mother's voice, 'you're drunk. Where's that other reprobate?'

'Father went out for some air. He was… a little hot.'

'Out for some air! In the freezing fog! It's nearly December, and your father steps out for some air at midnight…' Her voice softened. 'James…'

'Yes?'

'I hope you won't be like your father. When you're married, I mean.'

This was the last straw; Father was the most equable of men, and yet here she was complaining about his temper! 'Frankly, Mother, I think you're exaggerating a little.'

We heard the front door opening.

'Ah, that'll be Elizabeth,' said Mother. 'Strange that I didn't hear John's car…'

Father burst into the lounge. His overcoat was streaked with mud, as were his hands. His face was pale as he came lumbering towards us.

'Edward!' cried Mother. 'There's blood on your hands! Have you fallen? Oh, you poor dear, whatever has happened?'

'I think Arthur is dead,' he said, 'but I can't be sure. Quick, we've got to call a doctor.'

7

THE GIFT OF UBIQUITY

The violent assault on Arthur coincided with the strange disappearance of Henry. The general consensus was that one of their violent quarrels had turned physical; Henry had lost control and beaten his father, then, believing him dead, had fled into the night.

Fortunately, that evening my own father had the bright idea of taking a walk along the path that leads into the woods – in other words, the path that separates the White and Darnley properties. It was sheer good fortune that caused him to stumble across his friend's unconscious body, otherwise Arthur White would likely have gone undiscovered – he was lying just beyond the halo of light from the street lamp.

There could be no doubt that the assailant had wanted Arthur dead; his skull bore a gruesome double fracture. The ensuing investigation yielded little, except for the weapon – a rusted iron bar lying close to the victim's body – and the fact that Henry had vanished.

A week went by, and Arthur's condition slowly began to improve. The police waited impatiently for his account of events, as our friend was still unable to speak. And Henry was nowhere to be found.

There was nothing else for it. I needed to speak to the police. What I had seen a few hours earlier simply had to be reported.

The inspector in charge of the investigation had left us with his telephone number in case any new information should arise.

I dialled the number and waited.

'I want to speak with Inspector Drew,' I said in a confident tone of voice.

'And you are?'

'My name is James Stevens. I'm Mr White's neighbour and I have some important information to share.'

'"Important information"? Then you'd better join the queue, everybody's coming out of the woodwork today. You'll find him at your neighbours' place, the Latimers. They also had "important information" for him. I reckon he'll still be there.'

Five minutes later I was outside the Darnley home.

'Ah, James,' said John, ushering me through into the hall, 'somebody's seen Henry! The inspector is in the Latimers' lounge.'

I followed John upstairs without a word. Patrick and Inspector Drew were deep in conversation; they barely acknowledged my arrival. Victor greeted me wordlessly from his armchair, but Alice rushed over: 'James, have you heard the news? John must have told you about it. Come and sit down.'

Whenever I found myself in that young woman's company, a lump arose in my throat. I'm sure I wasn't the only one to perceive a hidden sensuality in her, of which she herself seemed unaware, but which nonetheless shone through whenever she moved, whenever she spoke in that soft yet husky voice, whenever she looked at you with those eyes that could be both fiery and frosty.

She took me by the arm and sat me down beside her husband. When she spoke, the two men immediately fell silent. 'Inspector, this is James Stevens, one of Henry's friends.'

'Good evening, young man. We are already acquainted, Mrs Latimer.'

'Of course,' said Alice with a vague smile. 'I must be losing my mind.'

'Fetch us some coffee, Alice, will you?' said Patrick. Though his tone was always friendly, there was something odd about him. He was almost too perfect, with his fair hair and deep blue eyes; his physique; his manners; the suave way in which he expressed himself. I tended to forget that he was an insurance salesman – a profession requiring perfect presentation. Really, I think I was just jealous of his beautiful wife.

'Mr Latimer,' the inspector went on, 'let's run through your statement again. This morning you drove your wife into London to do some shopping. Around noon, you went to Paddington Station to catch a train; you had some clients to see, and you were planning to return later. You were standing on the platform at exactly 12.30... and that's when you saw him.'

'That's right,' said Patrick. 'He had a sort of hunted look; he was extremely nervous, hoping nobody would notice him. But it was him, there's no doubt about it. I'm absolutely positive.'

'May I know who it is you're talking about?' I asked.

'We're talking about your friend, young man. Your friend who has been on the run for a week. Henry White.'

'But that's impossible,' I asserted. '*I* saw him at exactly the same time – on the platform at Oxford Station. That's what I came over to tell you.'

Taking advantage of the stunned silence, I continued: 'It was 12.30 precisely, I can assure you. He obviously hadn't shaved for several days, he was pacing about nervously, looking very anxious. But it was him. It was Henry. When he saw me, he turned to run. But then he changed his mind and came over to me. "People are just too cruel," he said. "I'm leaving." And then he walked away.'

Inspector Drew crushed out the cigarette he had just lit and sat back in silence. He looked at each of us in turn, then said, 'Somebody must have made a mistake.'

Patrick was thoughtful. 'I might misremember a conversation from time to time, but my eyes never deceive me.'

'James,' Alice interjected, 'you must have got it wrong. Henry was in London at 12.30. He was looking edgy and frightened, but it was definitely him.'

I shook my head. 'I'm sorry to contradict you, Alice, but I've known Henry since we were children. I saw him with my own eyes at 12.30, on the platform at Oxford Station.'

Before we could dispute the matter further, Inspector Drew cut in sharply, 'Enough! First Henry disappears without a trace, then we have *two* Henrys on our hands, though neither of them hangs around for very long. Which means I'm unable to charge him with the attempted murder of his father.'

Suddenly, the telephone rang.

Alice answered. 'It's for you, Inspector.'

He took the receiver from her and barked, 'What now?'

He hung up a moment or two later, looking annoyed. He had scarcely said a word. 'Mr White has regained consciousness,' he said, placing a fresh cigarette between his lips. 'My men have just finished questioning him. His version of events certainly complicates matters. According to him, he stepped out of the house at a quarter to midnight for a stroll. He paused on his doorstep when he glimpsed a shadowy figure heading towards the woods. Nothing unusual there, you might think. But the figure, he claims, was carrying a body on its shoulder.

'And so Mr White courageously set off in pursuit of the figure... but lost sight of it in the fog. He doesn't remember anything after that. He didn't recognise the figure, the body it was carrying or his attacker.'

PART TWO

1

A DANGEROUS ENCOUNTER

It was three years since Henry's disappearance. Had he run away to start a new life in America? Was he swinging from the trapeze in a travelling circus somewhere? Perhaps he was dead?

Inspector Drew certainly favoured the latter hypothesis. After taking Arthur White's statement, the investigator concluded that the body the 'shadow' had carried over its shoulder was Henry. The police scoured the woods with a fine-tooth comb, but turned up nothing.

Certainly the inspector's reasoning was questionable; after all, hadn't Henry been seen alive and well a week after the attack on his father, in not one but two different locations? To believe that, though, was to believe in almost anything. Even ghosts.

Last year, John set up his own business, opening a garage in the village. It was a risky enterprise, but certainly not as risky as proposing marriage to my sister. However, he did both.

The Latimers remained as tenants in the Darnley house, and now seemed to be very well off. The lovely Alice was certainly doing excellent business as a medium — her reputation had spread to the farthest reaches of the county and beyond.

As for Arthur White, it seemed that he was finally coming to terms with the grief at the loss of his wife and his son's disappearance. He immersed himself in his work, and spent most evenings in the company of Victor and the Latimers. He was currently working on a novel about spiritualism, which was to be entitled *The Land of Fog*. A rather inelegant title, in my view; I would have favoured *Mistland* or something like that. In fact, I suggested that to him and he told me he would think about it.

Village life had settled back into its regular routine again and the strange events of three years ago faded from memory.

But *were* they 'strange events'? After all, each could be explained if one were so inclined. Consider the death of Mrs Darnley: acute cases of psychosis are certainly rare, but not as rare as we like to think. Pick up a newspaper and see for yourself.

And the phantom footsteps? They might have been anything – even a tramp taking refuge in the attic. John had claimed someone was walking about in a room along the topmost corridor, but nobody was found. Let's be sensible about it: John must have misplaced the sounds, the tramp was in the attic itself. He never did search it, after all.

As for the simultaneous sightings of Henry in Oxford and London, somebody must have made a mistake – there could be no other conclusion. Whether it was the time of the identification or the sighting itself, somebody got it wrong.

What else is there? The late Mrs White providing the answer to her husband's question? Again, the solution is self-evident: some sort of collusion between Alice Latimer and Arthur White. And why? Simple: publicity. After all, she was a medium and he was an author – both adept self-publicists.

All these phenomena were explicable. The events that occurred three years later, however, were not.

'I have a small favour to ask of you, James. We need a trustworthy witness; a young, sensible fellow in full possession of his faculties.'

A few hours earlier, Arthur had invited me to visit him for a reason that he was unwilling to specify over the telephone.

And so I sat with him in his drawing room on that November afternoon in 1951.

He paced the room thoughtfully, his pipe clenched at the corner of his mouth.

I cleared my throat. 'I'm very flattered. But surely John meets the necessary criteria?'

'Victor already asked him,' Arthur explained, 'but John is too busy with work. So there will be five of us present this evening: you, Victor, the Latimers, and me.'

'Perhaps, Mr White, you could explain what this is all about?'

He paused in front of the French windows and contemplated the sight of the moor wreathed in mist, with its stark, skeletal trees. After a silence, he spoke.

'Last night, Alice had one of her fits. Well, she went into a trance, but it wasn't like before. She stayed that way for most of the evening. And she spoke. Unfortunately, Patrick couldn't catch everything she said, but he's convinced that it was a visitation. A visitation… in the haunted room.'

Arthur stopped to fill his pipe. He lit it, took a few puffs, then lowered his head and continued, 'On the one hand, these phenomena are not common, though they tend to be quite ordinary – not dangerous. This time, though, the circumstances were rather different. The Darnley house seems to be haunted by a particularly vindictive presence. Alice has been experiencing visions of a woman whose body is covered with stab wounds, and whose blood is spilling out of the open veins in her wrists. Just like Mrs Darnley.

'But that's not all. This spirit is in the grip of a blazing fury. Her eyes are aglow with hatred, she is crying out for revenge, pointing an accusatory finger at an invisible enemy…' He closed his eyes, concentrating hard, then added, 'The house is haunted by a vengeful spirit, who cannot rest until she receives justice. It's the only explanation for what's been going on.'

Arthur glanced around furtively, then drew closer to me and said in a low voice, 'Will you keep this between us, James?'

I nodded.

'Patrick has been speculating that Mrs Darnley did not actually commit suicide.'

Knowing what was coming next, I shuddered.

'He thinks she was murdered.'

'Ridiculous,' I commented.

'It seems that way, I grant you. But just imagine for a moment that there's a killer out there with the wherewithal to bolt a room from the outside. Everything about Mrs Darnley's death suggests murder – except for that bolt. The fact that the door was locked on the inside is the only obstacle to the murder theory. But a clever killer might be able to…'

'How? It's impossible.'

'I'm not sure I agree. I read a novel once where just such a trick was used. In it, the killer slid a double thread through the keyhole and looped it around the bolt handle. The trick was that he had slid a pin into the doorframe inside the room, and used it as a pulley. So he tugged on the double thread from outside and it pulled the bolt across. Then he let go of one end of the thread and pulled tightly on the other end. The pin, of course, was tied to the thread, and so, with a single sharp tug, that was it. There was no trace left – except for the single, insignificant hole in the doorframe, left by the pin.'

'Ingenious,' I said admiringly.

'Highly ingenious, though I've come up with another trick. This one is much more difficult to execute, but I think it's feasible. If the killer threw a hard rubber ball into the room just before pulling shut the door, he could predict its course as it bounced off the walls and ceiling. Therefore, with a careful aim he could cause it to hit the bolt and drive it into its housing.'

This theory left me paralysed with dread.

Arthur smiled slyly. 'You're afraid that I suspect Henry, aren't you? No, don't worry, my son is incapable of hurting a fly, and in any case he wasn't even ten years old at the time.'

Though Henry had been missing for three years with no sign of him whatsoever, Arthur still firmly believed that his son was alive. He avoided talking about him but, whenever he did, it was always in the present tense, as though Henry were still living under his roof.

'However,' Arthur continued, 'I must admit, it was his skill at juggling that suggested the possibility. Someone could easily have spotted him while he was practising one of his tricks and decided to learn it themselves, albeit for a more sinister purpose.'

There was a silence. I would have rejected this theory out of hand had I not once caught Henry pulling off just such a trick.

Arthur interrupted my train of thought. 'What I wanted to show you is that Patrick's theory *could* be true. In fact, I'll go so far as to call it a probability. Yes, Mrs Darnley was murdered. A horrific murder, perpetrated by a diabolical assassin. But it will not go unpunished. The time for atonement has arrived. Vengeance has spread its wings like a bird of prey, and prepares to swoop down on the guilty party, claws bared...'

I listened, fascinated by this disturbing flight of macabre lyricism. Arthur let his words hang in the air for a moment, then he looked me in the eyes and said in a deep, persuasive voice, 'That is why we are so afraid of this spirit. We fear it will attack any of us in its thirst for vengeance...' His voice grew more compelling still. 'It's up to us to take the initiative.'

'Take the initiative?'

'Yes. Tonight we are going to draw the spirit out, to urge it to speak... and at the same time to identify Mrs Darnley's murderer.'

'Where do you intend to conduct this experiment?'

Fear flickered in Arthur's eyes as he answered, 'At the scene of the crime. The room at the end of the corridor in the converted attic.'

Mad! They were all quite mad. I sat in shock, silent for a long moment, before asking as neutrally as I could muster, 'So you are expecting the spirit to materialise tonight. What form will it take?'

'Human, of course. We shall see Mrs Darnley again tonight.'

'Unless, of course,' I said jocularly, 'it delivers the murderer to you in the form of a corpse.'

Arthur's expression darkened. 'The experiment is dangerous, we are quite aware of that.'

'And how do you intend to go about it?'

'One of us will settle in the haunted room. Naturally, the room will be sealed. And, every half-hour, we will knock on the door to check that all is well. We need an independent witness to observe as the seals are broken. Otherwise it would be possible for some trickery to take place.'

'Who?'

'What do you mean, who?'

'Who is the one to be sealed up in the room?'

'First, we thought of Victor. But alas, he has a weak heart. Alice volunteered, in spite of her unease, but Patrick wouldn't hear of it. So he is going to do it himself.'

'Frankly,' I said, shaking my head, 'I don't know what to think…'

Arthur stared at me for a long while, then asked, 'May we count on your attendance?'

There was tension in the air. It was all going to end badly, I was convinced of it. All the same, I nodded.

2

THE HAUNTED ROOM

I PACED UP AND DOWN MY BEDROOM. I was on edge; the agony of waiting had caused my stomach to knot tensely, and my body stippled with sweat. With a trembling hand I stubbed out what must have been my twentieth cigarette, drew a handkerchief from my pocket and dabbed at my forehead.

Face it, James: you're terrified! The pale face staring back at me from the mirrored wardrobe door told me all I needed to know. I turned away from it and looked at my watch. Nine o'clock. Time to go.

I left the house and walked steadily towards the Darnley place. It was shrouded in a heavy yellow fog, with only the menacing points of its gables visible in the twilight. To fortify myself I started whistling a catchy little melody – not that it did much good.

Well, here goes. I pushed open the gate, which squealed in protest. I shuddered, my breath hitching in my throat. *Pull yourself together, for heaven's sake!* Traversing the driveway and mounting the stone steps, I paused for a moment and pressed the doorbell.

Alea iacta est. No turning back now.

Victor admitted me to the house. 'You're the last to arrive,' he said, offering a clammy hand.

'Is John here?'

'No, he's swamped with work. It's a pity.'

I looked him in the face, and could not believe what I saw. Victor had grown younger. His posture was more upright, and he wore a tasteful, elegant suit of cheviot tweed with a shirt and tie that matched perfectly – an ensemble which clearly dated back to the halcyon days of his material prosperity. With the silver hair at his temples, his robust complexion, and courtly manners, he was positively handsome. His eyes gleamed with foolish hope. This was a man deeply in love, who could not wait to see his beloved again after a lengthy separation.

Startled, I ventured, 'Will he be joining us later?'

'No,' he answered. 'John won't be able to leave work before midnight. He's working on some emergency repairs for a fussy customer.'

I did not comment. Naturally, John's work kept him very busy, but he usually managed to keep his Saturday evenings free. This was partly thanks to Elizabeth's influence; she liked to keep her husband close at hand. She certainly took after Mother in that regard.

While my sister and I had little in common, I couldn't help but concur when she said to me some time before they were married: 'Do you realise, James, that John wants us to go and live with his *father*? In that dreadful house? I threatened to call off the wedding unless he changed his mind.'

On reflection, that was just about the only time she and I were in agreement. Except on her choice of husband – she was lucky to have battened onto a chap like John. His garage was on the main road, beside the inn, and Fred had been good enough to rent out the upper floor to them. While this cupboard-like living space consisted only of a kitchen and a bathroom, it nonetheless had one significant advantage going for it: the place was not haunted; there were no phantom footsteps in the night.

'Come in, James. Let's go through to the others.'

Stifling a sigh, I trailed behind my host. Since John moved out, the house had grown even more sinister. The gloomy hallway and the dim light from the top of the stairs did not help matters.

Victor began to climb the staircase and I followed, resisting a wild urge to turn and make a run for it.

With one arm braced against the mantelpiece, Patrick attempted gently to extricate himself from his wife's clutches as we approached. 'We can't back out now,' he told her.

'But this is madness, darling,' Alice protested, clinging to him. 'It's far too dangerous.'

'I don't see why,' commented Victor. 'Eleanor has always been the kindest, gentlest of souls and, frankly, I doubt there is any reason to fear…'

Alice stared at the flickering tongues of flame in the hearth and said slowly, 'I have encountered your wife before, Victor. And I can tell you there is nothing of earthly kindness left in her. Her eyes burn with a yellow fire. They have no irises, just two black slits… She wants vengeance, brutal vengeance… She won't rest until she slaughters the coward who murdered her… up *there*.' She pointed towards the ceiling, above which lay the haunted room. 'Patrick, my darling,' she went on plaintively, 'she might make a mistake – she might take *you* for the murderer, or…' her voice trailed off.

Patrick studied his wife for a moment, then strode away from her towards the centre of the room, hands behind his back, his expression thoughtful.

'Mr White,' he said, 'did you remember to bring the…?'

'Of course,' replied Arthur, extracting a small velvet bag from the inside pocket of his jacket. He opened it and took out a small coin, which he showed to each of us in turn. 'This coin,' he continued, with the pride of an enthusiast sharing the jewel of his collection, 'is, you might say, unique. I did just as you asked: I selected it at the very last moment before leaving home to come here. And I can assure you, you won't find the like of it anywhere in the country.'

'Is this the coin you're going to use to seal the room?' I asked.

'The very same,' Patrick smiled, before glancing at his watch. 'Twenty-five past nine. We'd better get started. Darling, you may set up the equipment now.'

Alice examined him for a long moment, as though endeavouring to engrave his features in her memory, before seizing the candelabra from the table, taking the coin from Arthur, and leaving the room.

Patrick said, 'As soon as I am locked in the room, you will come up to check on me every half-hour or so. You will tap gently on the door; I will then advise you whether or not the spirit has manifested. There's no heating up there,' he added with a smile, 'so, if we don't produce any results after three or four hours, I think we may consider the experiment conclusive.'

'And what if there's no answer when we knock on the door?' I asked, panicking at the very thought of it.

'Well,' said Patrick sardonically, 'then perhaps my wife is right, and the spirit has vented its ire on me…'

'Not possible,' said Victor, beginning to display signs of impatience. 'Eleanor is incapable of hurting anybody.'

A heavy silence descended. Patrick began to grow nervous, pacing the room and muttering, 'What the hell is she up to? Dear God, it's been well over five minutes…'

The door opened and Alice appeared, pale as a wraith.

'Ah. Good. Up you go,' Patrick ordered, running a hand through his fair hair. 'I'll join you in a moment. I just need to put on my coat. It's chilly, after all. Now where did you put it, Alice?'

'Don't you remember, darling? You hung it on the coat rack at the bottom of the stairs.' Alice froze with a strange expression on her face. She seemed consumed by an unspeakable fear; a contagious dread which had taken hold of her entire audience – except Victor.

We left the room in silent procession. Patrick went downstairs to retrieve his coat; when he was out of sight, Alice beckoned us to follow her up the steps towards the attic. The lights from below barely illuminated the upper landing. A very small landing, in fact. In front of us was a blank wall; to the right, a door leading to the attic proper; to the left, a door leading to that dingy, narrow corridor.

'Let's go,' murmured Victor, his voice trembling with emotion.

Alice opened the door onto the dank corridor, lit by a flickering glow at the far end. After a collective intake of breath, there was a moment of almost total silence. At the end of the windowless corridor hung a heavy curtain, to the left was a panelled wall, and along the right-hand side were those four doors. The last door was open, and it was from within that fourth room that the tremulous, mesmeric light was emanating, reflected in the white earthenware handles of the other three doors. We were positively hypnotised by it; it drew us towards the room which had witnessed such a dreadful tragedy.

Alice led the way, pausing by the open door to allow us entry to the room. One by one, we filed inside. On the bare floorboards stood the candelabra and a small cardboard box; nothing else. The walls and floor were bare, as was the ceiling – not even a lone electric bulb hung from it. The room was completely empty. A floor, a ceiling, four whitewashed walls, a door, and a small window opposite. That was all.

Victor walked towards the window, halting in the centre of the room. Underlit by the candles, his face betrayed his extreme distress. Arthur stepped towards him, placing a warm hand on his shoulder, and murmuring low, comforting words. I felt a pang of sympathy for these two men, united by misfortune.

'That's where Mrs Darnley was found,' Alice whispered in my ear.

I gave an impatient nod. I knew it well enough; better than she did, in fact. Then I turned and began to examine the door. Alice took me by the arm and led me away. She closed the door, throwing the bolt on the inside, and said to me, 'We've already examined the lock at length. I just don't see how a killer could have drawn the bolt from outside the room...'

The staircase creaked. Footsteps approached along the corridor.

'Patrick, at last!' said Alice, drawing back the bolt and opening the door.

Dressed in a long black coat with the collar raised around his ears, Patrick strode silently into the room. A felt hat, the brim tilted downward over his face, left only his chin visible. There was something odd about him. He looked hunched, his head tucked down between his shoulders, as though his body had somehow shrunk.

'Are you ready, darling?' asked Alice softly.

Patrick grunted and went over to the window.

Alice clearly wanted to say something else; her lips parted, but no words came out.

Leaning on the window sill, Patrick gestured imperiously towards the door. Victor grabbed the candelabra and the cardboard box, then signalled for us to follow him. Arthur and I did not need to be asked twice, but Alice left the room with some reluctance, after a significant hesitation. I tried to imagine how she must be feeling, leaving her husband in this room... this chilly room, in the dark. I wouldn't have switched places with Patrick Latimer for any money in the world.

When the door was closed, Alice called out, 'Are you all right in there, darling?'

Patrick grunted from within.

'Well,' said Arthur in a tone intended to convey calm and reassurance, 'time to put the seals on and wait.'

With her gaze still fixed on the door, Alice nodded. Behind that cluster of wooden boards, scarcely visible against the panelled wall, was the man she loved, on a mission to raise a malevolent spirit. She gave a heavy sigh, then reached into the cardboard box and pulled out a ribbon of about eight inches in length. She placed it across the thin gap between the doorframe and the door itself – just above the handle – and asked Arthur to hold it in position. Then she removed a single candle from the candelabra and used its wax to fashion a pair of seals, which she applied firmly to each end of the ribbon with Arthur's coin.

The haunted room was sealed; nobody could enter or exit without damaging those seals.

Victor, who held the candelabra, stood with his eyes closed and his lips moving wordlessly. The poor man was praying; praying this experiment would prove successful.

As for me, I no longer knew what to think. I was quite ready for some sort of extraordinary event, but the 'resurrection' of Mrs Darnley? Certainly not. My reason would not allow for it. There was something insane as well as uncanny in this bizarre story; something painfully real, too, in Victor's desperate struggle to regain his lost happiness.

We descended from the attic like a funeral procession, settling once again in the Latimers' drawing room. The wait was agony; time seemed to stand still. Alice sat in her armchair, anxiously gripping the armrests on either side. That evening she wore a black tunic tastefully embroidered with gold and silver thread, with a high collar and pagoda sleeves, and a skirt of the same hue. Her hair was pinned back severely and held in place by a black headband. A silver medallion on a thick chain hung over her breast. Although I was accustomed to seeing her in this theatrical attire, she looked different this evening; paler, and troubled. No doubt the circumstances had something to do with it.

After ten minutes, a low creak came from the stairs, making us all jump. Then another, then silence.

'Mr White,' said Alice, 'don't you think we ought to—?'

'Let's give it another ten minutes,' Arthur replied, looking at his watch. 'We've only been at it for a quarter of an hour.'

'By the way,' asked Alice after a pause, 'did you get your coin back?'

'Yes,' said Arthur, patting his breast pocket, 'you gave it back to me as soon as you were finished with it.' He extracted the coin and examined it by candlelight. 'A very fine coin indeed, dating back to—'

'*Eleanor,*' said Victor, rising from his seat. 'Eleanor is back. She is upstairs. In that room.'

'Ten minutes past ten,' said Arthur, clearing his throat. 'I'm going to take a look upstairs.'

Alice nodded gratefully and he took a candle from the candelabra and left the room. He returned a couple of minutes later, looking deeply concerned.

'Is everything all right?' Alice demanded.

Arthur's only response was a question: 'Have you any scissors?'

Alice rushed over to her dressing table and removed a pair from one of the drawers. 'Here,' she said, 'but what is the—?' Then she noticed the strange look on Arthur's face; her eyes grew wide and her hand fluttered to her mouth.

'Eleanor is back. Eleanor is back,' Victor was chanting, his face lighting up.

'Come with me,' Arthur instructed.

We returned to the attic.

'Patrick! Patrick, darling!' Alice cried, hammering frantically on the door to the haunted room. 'Answer us, please!'

'Let's not panic,' said Arthur. 'It might be any number of things – he could have fainted, for instance. All the same, I think it would be best to remove the seals, just to be on the safe side.' He took the candelabra from Victor and brought it close to the door so that he might examine the ribbon and the two wax seals.

'Untouched,' he said with a sigh. 'Nobody has tampered with this door.' Then, with the scissors he sliced the ribbon down the middle. He gripped the door handle, closed his eyes, drew in a deep breath, and finally exhaled, 'Very well.'

He hurled open the door and candlelight spilled into the room. At the sight of the body lying in the centre of the floor, Alice gave an inhuman scream and collapsed like a rag doll – Victor put an arm round her, just about managing to keep her upright.

A deathly silence descended. Paralysed with dread, we stared at Patrick's body, which lay face-down in the very spot where Eleanor Darnley had died years before. The handle of a knife protruded from the middle of his back.

Arthur approached the body and knelt beside it. Patrick's arms were crossed underneath him, with one hand protruding. Arthur gripped it, feeling for the pulse, then shook his head. 'He's dead.'

He went over to the window and examined it, but it remained sealed.

'Nobody could have got into this room,' he said in a low voice. 'We have to face facts – something supernatural is going on here.'

'But Eleanor…' Victor stammered, still holding Alice upright. 'Eleanor couldn't have done this…'

Arthur seemed suddenly to realise the gravity of the situation. 'We were fools even to attempt this experiment,' he lamented, burying his face in his hands. 'Now we've got to get the police involved, though I doubt they'll concede the existence of a vengeful spirit. But, of course, there's no other explanation…'

He fell silent, his attention suddenly focused on the corpse. He knelt beside it, turning the dead man's head and removing the hat. His face fell; he got slowly to his feet, stepping backwards and leaning against the wall so he did not lose his balance.

Stunned, I approached the body myself. A shiver ran through me when I recognised Henry's face.

3
LOSING OUR MINDS

WE RETURNED TO THE LIVING ROOM IN a state of dazed consternation. I couldn't shake the horrifying thought that Mrs Darnley *had* returned for revenge on her murderer after all, and her murderer was *Henry*. It couldn't be true... and yet, no living person could have entered that sealed room.

And what about Patrick? Where was he? I tried in vain to get my thoughts in order. It was insane! A living nightmare.

A hand brandishing a glass of brandy entered my field of vision. I grabbed the glass and emptied it in a single gulp. My gaze then drifted over to the small sofa where Alice lay unconscious, before finally settling on Arthur. Victor offered him brandy too, but he shook his head; he was staring into space, all the life seemed to have drained out of him.

'The police will be here soon,' said Victor, sitting down beside me. 'What's happened to him is so awful... his wife, and now his only son... up there...'

'And Patrick?'

'I don't know. I can't bring myself to search the house yet. Let's hope that... James, I don't know what's happening to us, but it's dreadful. In a way, I'm glad Mrs Latimer hasn't regained consciousness yet. I don't know how I'm going to explain it to her...'

At that moment, the door swung open and Patrick tumbled into the room, clutching the back of his neck. 'What happened?' he stammered. 'Alice! Oh my God, is she...?'

He rushed to his wife's side. She finally began to come round, and clung to her husband, weeping. It was now time for explanations. I informed them of the horrors we had just experienced. For a moment, I feared Alice might faint again.

'Henry? Murdered? Up there?' Patrick cried. 'But...' He fell silent, went over to the table and poured himself two glasses of brandy, which he downed one after the other. 'I think I know what happened,' he said, lowering his head. We were hanging on his every word. 'When I went downstairs to fetch my coat,' he continued, 'someone attacked me. I was just heading for the coat rack, and then I blacked out. It was dark; I couldn't see who attacked me. Anyway, he must have taken my coat and hat, then gone up to the attic pretending to be me.'

'Of course!' I exclaimed. 'We never saw his face. We didn't hear his voice either, except for a few grunts. I thought there was something strange about him – particularly his gait. He was smaller than you, Patrick, he was about the size of...'

'Henry,' Alice concluded in a whisper.

'But what happened then?'

'Did you check the seals carefully?' asked Patrick.

Arthur broke his silence. 'Nobody could have entered the room. The seals were intact. You may see for yourself that they still are; I only cut the ribbon.'

When nobody commented on this, he added, 'The killer – if there was one – couldn't have obtained or produced a duplicate of the coin used for the seal, for the simple reason that nobody, including myself, knew which of the coins I was going to select. I didn't make my choice until eight-thirty, to be precise. Incidentally, my collection consists of over six hundred coins.'

Arthur was an extraordinary man. Even in the depths of his misfortune, he didn't lose his reason; he kept a cool head. Would the rest of us have been capable of that in his position?

'So Henry lets you lock him up in the room,' Patrick resumed, 'and...'

'We are in the presence of a supernatural murder,' Arthur cut in sharply. 'There's no other explanation. The only mystery is why Henry came back here at all. And... why he had to die.'

Nobody answered him.

'Are you sure it's really Henry?' Patrick asked. 'Maybe we ought to go up there and...'

'Let's wait for the police,' said Victor. 'They'll be here any moment.'

Just then, the doorbell rang.

'And here they are.'

The local police were naturally overwhelmed by this extraordinary crime, and so they immediately called in Scotland Yard. A chap called Chief Inspector Drew was put in charge of the investigation. He had risen through the ranks over the last three years; after several successes with particularly complex cases, the Yard considered him the best man for the job. A recent article about him in the press highlighted his uniquely *personal* method of catching criminals: Drew began by putting himself in the shoes of the culprit; he subjected suspects to intense interrogations, with all manner of questions unrelated to the case; he delved deep into their personal lives, in some cases all the way back to infancy, and compiled meticulous character studies. Because of all this, his colleagues at the Yard had nicknamed him 'The Psychologist'.

Before the body was taken away, it was identified as Henry. Arthur, however, would not accept his son's death. 'This man looks just like Henry,' he admitted, 'but it's not him.' The day after the tragedy, Drew arrived on the scene. The police had already examined the unbroken seals and the murder room. They searched in vain: there was no secret passage, no way of rigging the seals, and it was impossible to bolt the window from outside.

They questioned Arthur extensively about the coin used for the seal, but he was unequivocal: nobody could have predicted his choice and procured a duplicate in advance; even if they *could* have read his mind, it would have required extensive research and considerable time to create the copy. It was theorised that a copy could have been made using a cast, but expert opinion proved intractable: the prints on the two seals were made by Arthur's coin, not by any duplicate from a cast. There was still the possibility that a substitution had taken place *after* the door was bolted but *before* the seals were in place; a possibility Arthur refuted by stating that the coin had not left his pocket until he removed it himself – he had checked it frequently. Arthur also had an irrefutable alibi: between nine o'clock and ten (the approximate time of the murder, supplied by the police surgeon) he had not been left alone.

Of course, Arthur *could* have committed the murder with the aid of an accomplice – the only rational explanation for this 'impossible crime'.

A father murdering his son is not unheard of, but in this case there was no hint of a motive. An act of insanity? No, Arthur was of perfectly sound mind. So, the police were tearing their hair out in frustration by the time Chief Inspector Drew arrived. He had changed a great deal over the preceding three years; his face betrayed a quiet self-assurance, and the superior smile of a man who believed that he – and only he – knew the truth.

Following an examination of the crime scene, he reached the following conclusion: 'If all the witnesses are telling the truth, there are only two possibilities. Mr White murdered his son with the help of an accomplice, but I don't believe that's what happened. It's too obvious. The second, while far-fetched, remains within the realm of probability: after three years' absence, Henry returns to his village and pays a visit to the Latimers, or the Darnleys, whichever you like. He conceals himself in the downstairs hall, knocks Mr Latimer unconscious, steals his coat, heads up to the attic and allows himself to be locked in that room, all while pretending to be Mr Latimer. For the moment, let's not trouble ourselves with the motive for this bizarre behaviour. Then he opens the window and admits the murderer. Accessing the window from outside seems impossible at first glance, but it can be done by climbing out of an adjacent room and heading across the roof. The murderer then stabs Henry in the back, and leaves via the same route. In his final moments before death, Henry closes and bolts the window. And it is this single, seemingly incomprehensible gesture that gives this murder its "supernatural" appearance. These "impossible crimes" always have a simple explanation.'

'What an excellent meal. Sublime! Never in all my life have I tasted anything so…'

'Don't exaggerate, James. You're overdoing it. I might even think you're making fun of me,' Elizabeth protested.

'James isn't exaggerating, my dear,' John intervened. 'On the contrary, I think he underestimates your culinary talents. The best French restaurants would pay a fortune to have you in one of their kitchens.'

Elizabeth looked at us incredulously, unsure what to think.

Two days after the tragedy, my sister had invited me to dinner. This occurred so seldom, it was obvious she wanted to hear all the gory details of that infamous, tragic evening. She made me tell the story twice, interrupting frequently with 'James, stop! It's just too horrible, I can't bear to hear any more…' before immediately continuing, 'What then?'

'What do you think, John?' Elizabeth asked casually.

'I already told you, the cuisine is exceptional.'

'I'm talking about Henry's murder.'

'I don't know,' John replied with a curious look. 'In the village they aren't talking about a "haunted room" any more – they're talking about a "deadly room". Some of my customers have even suggested that Henry murdered my mother, and that her spirit came back for revenge. But I don't believe in ghosts. I *am*, however, beginning to think there might be a homicidal maniac on the loose, and that perhaps my mother was killed after all...'

'Oh, John, please! That's enough,' said my capricious sister. 'And to think you wanted me to live in that house! But why on earth would anybody want to murder your poor mother? And why was Henry killed?'

'Maybe he knew who killed your mother, John,' I suggested.

'If that were the case,' said John, glancing at me sideways, 'surely he would have been eliminated a long time ago.'

'True.'

There was a pause.

'The papers have reported the murder, but they're keeping quiet about the bizarre circumstances,' said Elizabeth, who was decidedly well-informed.

'Of course,' I sighed, 'the police don't want the rumour mill going out of control. Their competence has already been called into question lately.'

John nodded. 'And what do you make of Inspector Drew's hypothesis?' he asked abruptly.

'His idea that Henry closed and bolted the window in his dying moments? It's ridiculous. It doesn't hold water.'

'*I* think it makes sense,' my sister interjected confidently. Vexed by our silence, she persisted, 'Henry was rather vain, I can quite see him playing one last trick on us. He wanted to go out on a high; to have a death worthy of the great illusionist he imagined himself to be. I think Inspector Drew has hit the nail on the head. He understands Henry's psychology very well indeed. They don't call him "The Psychologist" for nothing.'

I opened my mouth to reply, but was dissuaded by a look from John.

'Have they checked everyone's alibis?' he asked me.

But Elizabeth didn't give me time to answer. 'There's only one person without an alibi,' she said.

John looked at her thoughtfully. 'Ah,' he finally said, 'I see. You mean to say that Patrick might have...'

'I'm not talking about Patrick,' Elizabeth replied. 'I'm talking about *you*, John.' She pointed accusingly. 'You were alone at the garage until midnight, after all.'

John smiled. 'A very astute observation, my dear. But in that case, it's worth noting that *you* don't have an alibi either.'

She got to her feet, trembling slightly. 'Are you accusing me? Your own wife?' she snapped, choking back her rage.

I held up my hands in a gesture of appeasement. 'Enough! You'll have plenty of time to squabble after I've gone. Speaking of which, I'd better be on my way. It's nearly eight-thirty, and I need to stop by at Mr White's place.'

'Is it really as urgent as all that?' asked John. 'Couldn't you see him tomorrow?'

'Actually, it's not Mr White who asked for the meeting. It's Inspector Drew. I think he has some more questions.'

'Poor Mr White,' Elizabeth commented. 'Don't you think the police ought to spare him the inconvenience, after everything he's been through?'

'I wouldn't worry about him,' I said. 'He isn't brooding; he's quite convinced that the body found in that room is not his son, even though everyone else was positive. Anyway...'

With that, I thanked them again for the excellent meal and took my leave.

Outside, a biting cold and a pale moon were my only companions as I scurried along the deserted street. As I walked, I recalled the night of the tragedy, running through the events in chronological order. There was something strange that I could not quite pin down. I could say *when* it occurred, but not *why* it was bothering me. It was our second climb up the staircase to the attic: we entered the corridor, we knocked on the door… and no answer came. We removed the seals… we opened the door… we found the body…

No, that's not it. I'm getting carried away. The curious impression came to me just as…

Ah! If only I could remember. Was it a gesture? A word? A sight? A sound? There's no point racking my brains; it will come to me as soon as I stop thinking about it.

I had no way of knowing then that if I had just managed to work out what I had seen, I would inevitably have uncovered the diabolical method employed by the murderer. And, as a result, another monstrous crime would have been prevented; a crime whose motive has never been made public, and for good reason.

You will soon see what I'm talking about. But I'm getting ahead of myself.

It was nearly quarter-past nine when Arthur finished recounting the night of the tragedy. He was so precise, and accurate on every point, that there was no need for me to interrupt him. Drew, who was sitting in a comfortable armchair with his arms folded over his chest, shook his head with a slight smile.

'I'm afraid that your account, while remarkably detailed, contains nothing new.' He turned his piercing gaze in my direction. 'What about you, Mr Stevens? Have you nothing to add? Perhaps a point that Mr White may have missed?'

'No,' I replied, lighting a cigarette so that I might look away from those two probing blue eyes. 'There's nothing to add; Mr White has recounted the evening perfectly, and since he and I were together the entire time, there's nothing else I can say.'

Arthur narrowed his eyes slightly, drawing a lungful of smoke from his pipe. 'This is the third time I've recounted these events in forty-eight hours,' he said. 'I imagine you know them well enough that you might have been there yourself.'

'Scotland Yard does not believe in ghosts,' Drew said abruptly.

'Everyone has a right to their beliefs,' Arthur retorted. After a pregnant silence, he continued, 'By the way, what about your theory that the dead man closed the window in his final moments, after the murderer was gone?'

Drew's eyes flashed, but he maintained a measured tone. 'It was an early theory, purely to demonstrate that the crime was not necessarily committed by a phantom. It's unlikely that events really transpired that way. For one thing, there were no fingerprints on the window handle. And for another, the medical examiner indicates it would have been impossible for your son to move about after receiving such a heavy wound.'

Arthur looked annoyed. 'For the last time, the dead man is *not* my son.'

Drew looked down at his shoes, with that same smile on his lips. 'Let's be reasonable, Mr White,' he said in a tone that was presumably intended to be conciliatory. 'Everyone who saw the body identified it as your son. I can quite understand that you're unwilling to believe it, but we must face facts.'

'Indeed, Mr White,' I said diplomatically, 'it was Henry. Believe me, if there were any room for doubt I would be the first to express reservations.'

Arthur was unmoved. A leaden silence descended as Drew slipped a cigarette between his thin lips, lit it and cleared his throat before continuing, 'This is a strange case, to say the least.'

'Quite,' I agreed. 'When a man is found murdered in a hermetically sealed room, the least one can say is that—'

'Yes, yes, but that's not my point,' Drew rejoined. 'Mr White, it's three years since you were attacked and left unconscious on the path outside this house, isn't that right?'

'Perfectly correct,' Arthur said with a note of annoyance in his voice. 'I even remember telling police at the time that I saw someone carrying a body into the woods just before I lost consciousness... though nobody seemed to think it was particularly important.'

Drew, in turn, seemed annoyed. 'What do you mean, not important? The woods were searched, no body was found, no disappearances were reported in the area. What else would you have had us do?'

'My *son* disappeared,' Arthur snapped. 'What do you call that?'

The fact that Arthur was a famous novelist no doubt persuaded Drew to remain calm. 'I was getting to that,' he said gently. 'Immediately after the attack, your son disappears. However, a few days later he reappears in two different places at the same time. This is extraordinary enough, but the story does not end there. He then manages to infiltrate a hermetically sealed room, and finds a way to get himself stabbed to death in there.' Drew was now struggling to contain himself. 'I might as well warn you, Mr White, the truth of this affair *will* come out, no matter who is responsible. I have never failed, and I don't intend to start now.'

The doorbell rang.

'That will be Victor,' said Arthur, getting to his feet. But he changed his mind. 'Ah, no, I've just heard a car pull up. It must be some other visitor. Excuse me for a moment, please.'

He left the room, and Drew and I remained there in silence, listening intently.

We heard what sounded like a cry of surprise, then a car engine starting up, and then nothing. Finally, there came a series of exclamations. When Arthur spilled back into the room, he looked to be weeping with joy. Behind him stood a dim silhouette, which became clear as it stepped into the light.

My heart stopped. My reason left me. It was Henry. Henry, in the flesh.

4

AN AUDIENCE WITH THE PSYCHOLOGIST

'Hello, James old man,' said my friend with a broad grin.

I hugged him tightly, then held him at arm's length to get a proper look at him. 'Henry! Is it really you?'

A tear formed at the corner of his eye, then sluiced down his cheek. 'It's good to see you again, James. Really, you've no idea,' he murmured, clearly moved. This was Henry all right; only he could speak with such tenderness.

'Inspector Drew,' said Arthur, dabbing at his eyes with a handkerchief, 'allow me to present my son, Henry.'

Drew, whose facial muscles were straining to produce a smile, spoke in honeyed tones that positively dripped with acid. 'Delighted, young man. Delighted.' He looked like the devil himself, plotting a terrible vengeance. His green eyes flashed and his face had taken on a curious hue, like an old man suffering a gallbladder complaint.

In my euphoria, I couldn't help but cry out, 'Henry's back!'

With the smile still frozen on his face, Drew bared his teeth. For a moment he looked as though he might unsheathe a set of claws and pounce on my friend to devour him whole. He contented himself, however, with a sneer.

'Henry,' I said in a voice I scarcely recognised, 'how—? Why—?'

My head was spinning and my knees buckled. I was immensely

glad of the armchair behind me. It must have been my obvious shock that provoked Arthur to action. Trembling with emotion, he made for the drinks cabinet.

'We must drink a toast to Henry's return!' he declared in a strident voice to mask his emotion. 'To Henry!'

There were a thousand questions I might have asked, but my throat felt constricted; I remained motionless in my seat, my mind refusing to focus. But there was nothing wrong with my eyes: Drew was studying Henry carefully; Arthur, his face aglow with joy, was filling four glasses to the brim; Henry had come over and slipped an arm around my shoulders.

Arthur downed his drink in a single gulp, closed his eyes thoughtfully, reopened them, and said, 'Three years. Why three years of silence, son?' His tone was solemn, and full of sorrow.

'Why indeed?' echoed Drew sardonically.

Henry hung his head, and did not reply.

'They said you were dead,' Arthur continued. 'I knew you weren't, but all the same... And who's this man that was found dead next door? Do you know about it, Henry? Have you seen it in the papers? They are all saying it was you...'

Henry looked each of us in the face, then nodded.

'Yes, just who *is* the dead man?' asked Drew with icy sweetness.

Hanging his head again, Henry paced up and down a little, before pausing and finally blurting out, 'He was my partner, an American named Bob Farr.'

'So you've been in America all this time?' Arthur asked, his eyes wide.

'Yes...' Henry paused. 'I... We... Among other things, we performed an escapology routine together. He was a circus acrobat when I met him. When we first clapped eyes on each other, it was like a bolt of lightning. We both realised instantly how useful our remarkable resemblance could be. What are the chances — two men who look identical, and happen to work in the same profession! We certainly made the most of it; we had huge success with our escapology act. We could appear and disappear at will, and the audience thought they were watching only one man! And now... Bob's dead.'

There was an agonised silence.

Arthur, who had managed to control himself so far, suddenly broke down in tears.

'Bob Farr is dead,' said Drew, his eyes reflecting the twin curls of cigarette smoke that coiled from his nostrils. 'Could you tell me, young man, what your partner was doing next door the evening before last?'

'No,' replied Henry, 'I can't tell you anything yet. No, not yet.'

'Not yet,' repeated Drew, examining the glowing tip of his cigarette with a Mephistophelean smile. 'Very well. In that case, perhaps you can tell me whether or not he had any enemies? He was murdered, after all.'

Henry shook his head.

'All right, all right,' Drew continued. 'By the way, have you heard about the strange circumstances surrounding your partner's death?'

'I read it in the papers. He was found in the attic, stabbed to death.'

'Yes,' Drew concurred, 'that's what the papers said. They're not wrong, but they left out certain details. Certain details which I will be glad to explain to you. But first, when did you arrive from America?'

'I set foot on English soil a few hours ago. I took the first train to Oxford, and got a taxi from there.'

'Good. Very good, very good. Excellent.' Drew had taken a notebook from his pocket and was making notes. 'I won't ask your father to describe the tragic events, or your friend who is still clearly beside himself. I shall tell you the story myself.'

When he had reached the conclusion, the inspector asked

Henry, 'What do you make of that, young man? Since you are apparently an expert in sleight-of-hand, perhaps you can assist us. Any ideas what clever method the murderer used?'

Henry did not answer. His head was in his hands.

'Inspector,' he finally said, 'there's nothing I can tell you. Nothing… yet.'

Arthur, who was studying his son anxiously, got up from his chair and spoke to Drew. 'Inspector, I don't mean to be rude but… well, I haven't seen my son for three years. I'm sure you can understand.'

Still watching Henry, Drew got slowly to his feet. 'I understand perfectly, Mr White.' He gathered his belongings and wrapped himself in his long, beige scarf and elegant overcoat. Then he approached Henry with a feline smile. 'A word of advice, young man. Don't stray too far from home for the time being. And remember there are no secrets when Inspector Drew is around. I shall come and see you tomorrow, for a friendly little chat.'

With that, Drew bowed stiffly and withdrew. The front door slammed behind him.

'What a curious fellow,' said Henry after a pause.

'Put yourself in his place,' said Arthur. 'He has an incredibly strange case on his hands. And please, my boy, don't pretend you don't know what Bob Farr was doing here.'

Another silence descended, and I was the one who broke it. 'Henry, did you know somebody attacked your father the night you disappeared? And a few days later I saw you at Oxford Station, while the Latimers saw you at the exact same moment at Paddington? I realise now they must have seen Bob Farr instead. Please, Henry, tell us everything. Don't stand there in silence. The inspector's gone, you can come clean with us now!'

Henry gave us a pleading, tearful look. 'Father. James. Don't ask me yet. Don't ask any questions. One day soon, I'll tell you everything. You'll understand it all then. But I'm begging you, please don't ask me any more questions. I need some time to think.'

Early the following morning, Drew returned to question Henry. The interview didn't last long, and the inspector left the house a quarter of an hour later, looking furious, with his head bowed. Watching with my nose pressed against the bedroom window, I could tell instantly what had happened: Henry had faced down the furious Drew, and hadn't said a word.

The day passed as I had expected; the whole village was taken aback to learn of Henry's miraculous resurrection. By the time Mother returned from shopping, everybody knew; the baker, the grocer, the butcher – to name just a few – had only one word on their lips: Henry.

I didn't set foot outside that day, and remained locked in my room trying to organise the countless tangled thoughts cluttering my brain. That evening, John and Elizabeth stopped by and my sister, the inquisitor in petticoats, did her best to get the story out of me. I told her everything I knew, which wasn't much. John and my parents were clearly uneasy, and had little to say. Of course they were delighted that Henry was alive, it was wonderful news, but we were all wondering what was going to happen next – the tension in the air was palpable. And, indeed, it would not be long before the spectre of death fell across the village once again.

Ever since Henry's return, Inspector Drew had not strayed far. He was constantly on the prowl, knocking on doors, firing questions at the neighbours. Naturally my parents and I received a visit. He questioned us at length about Henry; about his childhood, his interests, his character. The Psychologist was on the case.

The press remained relatively circumspect. There were two or three paragraphs on the incorrect identification of the corpse, but nothing further. Naturally we had expected it to be splashed across the headlines: *Locked-Room Murder! Son of famous author returns from the dead!* Arthur clearly carried a lot more influence than I had thought.

The following evening, I went to see Henry. He spoke to me at great length about his time in America, about his shows with Bob Farr, and how the incredible resemblance between them had mystified audiences everywhere they went. I asked him what he was planning to do now.

'I don't know, James,' he answered. 'I need to take stock. But I just don't know.'

When I brought up the taboo subject of Bob Farr's murder, all he said was 'Later, James. I need time to think.'

Then came that infamous evening. An evening I will never forget, like everyone else who happened to be there – particularly Chief Inspector Drew.

It was almost a week since Henry's return. At Drew's request, Arthur had gathered everyone involved in the affair at his home that icy November evening. The fireplace crackled, but it made little difference to the frosty atmosphere in that room. There was also the matter of the two uniformed police officers Drew had brought with him – they also cast a certain chill. Particularly since they were stationed by the door, as though to prevent us from leaving.

The Latimers sat side by side on the sofa. Alice looked pale, and clung to her husband for support. He, too, seemed rather uncomfortable. To their right, John and Elizabeth sat positively quivering with anticipation. Arthur and Victor were settled in armchairs, while Henry and I sat by the fireplace. Henry looked rather elegant in a grey velvet suit, with a burgundy bow tie that contrasted boldly with his pale blue shirt. With his elbows propped on his knees and his gaze fixed on the ground, he wrung his hands anxiously.

Chief Inspector Drew stood staring into the fireplace, his hands behind his back. Then he turned abruptly to face us all, and spoke theatrically.

'Ladies and gentlemen, the mystery surrounding the death of Bob Farr is now solved. Now that you are all gathered here, I may tell you that the Machiavellian assassin is in this very room.'

There was a ripple of terror among the guests, but nobody said a word. Drew calmly lit a cigarette, inhaled a few pulls of smoke, then continued, 'First, I must ask that none of you interrupt me. It may not seem that everything I am telling you is strictly relevant to the case, but I assure you now that it is. So even if what I am saying seems nonsensical, do not interrupt.'

Drew reached into his jacket pocket and produced a rubber ball which he began to bounce up and down in the palm of his hand. There was a devilish smile on his lips. He showed the little ball to his subordinates.

'Look at this,' he said, 'and tell me what you see.'

It was such a ridiculous question that nobody could bring themselves to answer it. Satisfied with our collective astonishment, he continued, 'This little ball is the murder weapon. Or rather, let's say it was used to create the most remarkable part of the illusion: the locked-room murder. I believe I am correct in saying that there are still some of you here who believe the crime was committed by a ghost.' He paused and replaced the ball in his pocket.

'Now, I do not categorically deny the existence of spirits. It would be foolish not to acknowledge certain phenomena which cannot be explained by earthly means. But when it comes to this particular case, one thing is for certain: we are dealing with a flesh-and-blood murderer. And a devilishly clever one at that.'

You could hear a pin drop in that room.

Drew picked up a purple-covered book from the mantelpiece. Leafing through it, his lips curled into a grin. Then he brandished the book and spoke in a deep, solemn voice. 'The story of the murder is contained in this book, down to the last detail.' He held the book in front of him. 'You would have to be blind not to see it. But then, I suppose my colleagues call me "The Psychologist" for a reason.'

To the astonishment of his audience, he revealed the title of the book: *Houdini and his Legend.*

'Let me tell you a little something about Houdini,' Drew continued, evidently very pleased with himself. 'I shall begin with his exploits, then move on to the psychology of the man himself. And I must reiterate, please do not interrupt.

'No doubt you are all familiar with Harry Houdini. The Handcuff King! The World's Greatest Escape Artist! The man who captivated audiences in the early years of this century, who mystified presidents and heads of state. His earliest triumph was in 1898, when the Chicago daily newspapers carried the headline: "Houdini, King of Handcuffs, challenges the Chicago Police Department to keep him handcuffed for more than one hour in a state prison cell."

'The police quickly took up the challenge. Thus Houdini was locked in a cell, under the watchful eye of a group of police officers. A crowd of reporters gathered in the prison director's office to see what would happen. They did not have to wait long because, mere minutes later, the door opened and Houdini entered the room, completely free from his bonds. Their amazement was short-lived, however, as one reporter accused Houdini of going into the cell with lock-picking equipment concealed on him. Houdini volunteered to repeat the experiment right away, this time undergoing a thorough search beforehand. The search was carried out by a doctor, who found nothing, and so Houdini returned to his cell – this time completely naked. His clothes were placed in another cell, which was also locked. The wait was even shorter this time, and when Houdini entered the director's office wearing his own clothes, his audience was astonished.

'Two years later, in 1900, Houdini travelled to England. From the beginning, his performances dazzled London society. Particularly the feat which concluded each show: he invited audience members to handcuff him, and guaranteed to free himself within minutes. He was challenged by Scotland Yard to escape from one of their own cells, in the headquarters of the most famous police force in the world! Naturally, Houdini could not resist the publicity, so he accepted the challenge. He was escorted along a corridor and asked to wrap his arms around a stone column, before his wrists were cuffed together. The policemen left him, gleefully confident that he would be unable to escape. They had scarcely taken a few steps when Houdini's voice came from behind them: "If you're going back to the office, wait for me, I'll come with you." They looked around and saw to their amazement that it was Houdini following them, entirely free from his restraints.

'This feat brought the American illusionist to new heights of fame. Londoners flocked in their thousands to see the man who had dared to challenge Scotland Yard. His European tour was a huge success; he filled vast theatres in places like Berlin, Dresden, Paris – even Moscow. He became a household name as a wizard with strange and terrifying powers, even performing for royalty.

'This spectacular European tour came to an end in Moscow, in 1903. You are probably familiar with the notorious armoured vehicle used to transport political prisoners to Siberia – a carriage with thick steel walls, drawn by four horses. It had only one tiny window, and a door which could only be locked or unlocked from the outside. Indeed, it could only be unlocked by a single key, which was held in Siberia. At first glance, it was entirely impossible to escape from this vehicle.

'In spite of this, Houdini accepted the challenge. After subjecting himself to the most rigorous body search of his entire career, he was locked in the carriage and sent to Siberia. Within an hour, he had escaped!

'Then he headed to the New World, performing in all the major cities of the United States. Every local police force received his business card, and he managed to escape from every single cell – most notably in Washington, where he freed not only himself but every prisoner in the place!

'But our man was not limited to this one type of exploit. He plunged into icy rivers with cuffs round his wrists and ankles, or with cannonballs chained to his feet! He could free himself from a straitjacket in minutes, sometimes while suspended upside-down ten storeys high! He was locked in a coffin, buried six feet below ground! He escaped from vaults and strong rooms! There was nothing and nowhere from which he could not escape: handcuffs, chains, straitjackets, ropes, prison cells, coffins, padlocked trunks, safes, post bags sealed with wax, and so on – nothing stopped him. And that's not all; he even made an elephant disappear, and walked through a brick wall.

'This great man who astonished the whole world died in October 1926, following a stupid accident. He invited a member of his audience to punch him in the stomach, and—'

'Inspector Drew,' Arthur cut in sharply, 'we are all familiar with Houdini. It's an interesting story, but is this really the appropriate time?'

Drew smiled. 'Houdini's life is directly linked to the murder of Bob Farr. I admit that I may have dwelt a little on the magician's exploits, so let's get to the heart of the matter: the psychology of Harry Houdini. Again, I would ask you not to interrupt me, and to listen carefully to what follows, because it contains the solution to the entire mystery.'

His audience sat in stunned silence.

After a pause, Drew continued, 'Harry Houdini, as you can probably guess, was a stage name. His real name was Erich Weiss. He was born prematurely on 6 April 1874. His place of birth is not known, but it is believed to be Budapest. From a young age he entertained his classmates with sleight-of-hand tricks, and supposedly his first experiments with a lock were on the door to the cupboard where his mother kept the sweets. At age seven, he went to the circus for the first time and, by the age of fifteen he had devised his own magic act, which he performed with a friend.

'Houdini was not born great; it was through intense training, passion for his art, an iron will, and boundless ambition, that he achieved greatness.

'Yes, his ambition knew no bounds; his entire brilliant career proves it. He had a continual need to break new ground, to constantly surprise his audience. This makes his psychology comparatively simple to understand – he was dominated by his pride and his ego. He was unafraid to risk his life at every turn, to surpass himself each time, with the sole aim of not disappointing his audience. It is easy to imagine him as a kind of petulant man-child. His attitude towards the fairer sex is curious too; he appears to have been both shy and remarkably jealous – groundlessly so – towards his wife. He was also extraordinarily devoted to his mother.

'In 1916, Houdini and his wife were travelling to Europe by ocean liner. One night, approximately half-way through their crossing, Houdini awoke in his cabin, afflicted by an inexplicable sorrow, and began to weep. He later learned that at that very moment, his mother had died of a heart attack.'

I almost jumped out of my seat. I recalled the death of Mrs White, and the way Henry seemed to have known of it at the precise moment it occurred. But Drew could not have known about that; it was a secret between Henry and me. Nonetheless, I began to see where Drew was going with all this: drawing parallels between Houdini and Henry. But to what end?

I glanced at my friend. Henry was no longer hanging his head, and had now fixed the inspector with a strange look.

'Houdini adored his mother,' Drew continued. 'He revered her, cherished her, showered her with gifts. Her death was the great tragedy of his life. He fell into fits of sorrow and despair that nothing on earth could alleviate. Naturally, he was unable to perform on stage. However, he eventually managed to overcome his grief by finding hope in a very curious place: the world of spiritualism. He tried a number of experiments in this field, but the repeated failure of his "communications" with his late mother turned his sorrow into fury, so he sought revenge on the spiritualists who had failed him. He showed no pity to the hoaxers, and unmasked numerous fraudsters with purported "powers".

'In spite of this, we cannot be sure of what he truly thought about spiritualism. Some claim that deep down he remained convinced of the existence of the supernatural. Indeed, on his deathbed he left his wife with a secret message which he planned to convey to her from the beyond. Bess Houdini died in 1943, and nobody knows whether or not Houdini had managed to contact her.'

Drew's lecture was over. He closed the book and cast a satisfied look at his audience.

'Don't you see?' he said.

Arthur rose from his seat. 'See what? There are certain similarities between my son and Houdini, I concede that. But what does it matter? Inspector, I'm afraid your reputation as

"The Psychologist" has gone to your head. You are finding subtleties where none exist!'

Drew's answer was a smile. He took a few steps up and down in front of the fireplace, before stopping to contemplate the hearth. 'Certain similarities…' he said softly. 'I have spent three long days interviewing Henry's friends, his family, his associates… We have talked about his childhood, his personality… I have learned a great deal in those three days.'

His smile was gone; his voice was low.

'And I think I can say that I know as much about Henry as every single one of you. But that's nothing special. It's all part of the job: psychology.

'Permit me, then, to go over a few of these so-called similarities between Henry and Harry Houdini. Both were born prematurely. That, in itself, is not unusual. From a young age, both amused their friends with sleight-of-hand tricks and lock-picking. Furthermore, both were regular visitors to the circus. Those two children shared the same desire: to astonish others, to dazzle them, to be the centre of attention at all times! Do you see it now? The extreme egotism? The pride?'

I was about to intervene, but Arthur White beat me to it. 'You are exaggerating, Inspector, you really are. This is something every artist has in common,' he added ironically.

The accuracy of this remark clearly irritated Drew. He turned around quickly, grabbed the book and produced a photograph which had been slipped between the pages. He showed it to the audience and declared triumphantly, 'Look closely at this photograph. It shows Harry Houdini. Does it remind you of anybody? Anybody in *this very room*?'

The resemblance to Henry was undeniable: the broad face, the hair parted down the middle, the same expression, the same bulky frame… but there must have been thousands of men who looked like that! Henry, who had been hanging onto the inspector's every word, looked eagerly at the photograph, absolutely fascinated. Nobody else seemed particularly interested.

Suddenly, Arthur began to laugh. It was a forced laugh that ended abruptly. 'This is beyond the pale, Inspector. If it's a joke, it's in very poor taste. I'm surprised that a man in your position would stoop to…'

'Mr White,' Drew said sharply, his eyes ablaze. He smiled sardonically, before continuing in more gentle tones. 'Mr White… or should that be Mr Weiss?'

Arthur leapt from his seat, his face pale. He stammered, 'How… how did you…?'

'Simply by doing my job. I conducted an investigation into everyone involved in this affair. Therefore I learned that you are of Hungarian origin, born in Budapest, and that your real name is Weiss… which you changed to White when you arrived in England at the age of twenty-one. Is all of this correct?'

Arthur gave a barely audible murmur. 'Yes.'

'Our inquiries did not produce much else. You are an orphan, that's all we were able to determine. Therefore, permit me to remind you of Houdini's real name: Erich Weiss, also a native of Budapest…'

'Inspector,' Arthur said tremulously, 'Weiss is a common name. The fact that I'm an orphan and never knew my parents doesn't prove… well, whatever it is you're trying to prove, for heaven's sake! That Henry has Houdini blood in his veins? So what if he does? And even if he *did*, what difference does it make to anything?'

'I'm getting to that,' Drew said calmly. 'It doesn't matter really whether Henry is actually related to Houdini or whether he is some kind of reincarnation…'

'A reincarnation?' Arthur barked. 'My son, a reincarnation? Inspector, this time you've really crossed the line…'

'Father,' Henry interrupted, 'please, let's listen to what the inspector has to say.'

Drew examined Henry for a moment before continuing. 'Young man, we have now reached the crux of the matter. You adored your mother… just as Houdini did. It was not a normal love between mother and son, but an excessive love, which plunged you into an abyss of pain when she died… just like Houdini. Sheer torment, and floods of tears which nothing could stem. You even contemplated suicide… Don't try to deny it, young man. I'm very well informed. Your despair has left a mark on everyone in the village. Houdini's love for his mother mirrored your own.

'But let's go back three years, and observe the sequence of events chronologically. At the beginning of September 1948, Mrs White is killed in a tragic car accident. Henry, as we have already discussed, sinks into a deep depression. A few weeks later, word begins to get around that Henry and his father quarrel frequently. This is more than a mere rumour; it's a fact. These altercations become increasingly violent, though nobody really knows why. And then, at the end of November, comes the attack on Mr White. When I say "attack", of course, what I really mean is "attempted murder". It was a miracle that he survived. And, by a curious coincidence, that very same instant Henry vanishes into thin air.'

He looked around briefly, before adding, 'You still don't see?'

The only answer was silence.

'Very well, very well,' he continued, 'then I'd better dot the "i"s and cross the "t"s. Henry couldn't come to terms with his mother's death. He began to act out. He was looking for someone to blame. And, of course, it was his father who had lost control of the car that night, and was therefore directly responsible for the death of his beloved mother. Henry could not allow that crime to go unpunished; his father was guilty, and therefore justice must be served.

'During one of these daily violent quarrels – Henry lambasting his father for causing his mother's death – Henry smashes in his father's skull with an iron bar. He believes he has killed him, and so goes on the run, seeking refuge with his friend Bob Farr. He convinces Bob to leave with him, and both men abandon England for America. A week later, when the two men are about to leave the country for good, they are planning to meet at Paddington Station. By a singular coincidence, both are glimpsed at exactly the same time: one at Oxford Station taking the train for London, and the other waiting for his friend. And they look so similar – identical, in fact – it might easily be believed that Henry had a doppelganger.

'As for Mr White, who claims to have witnessed a shadowy figure carrying a body off into the woods… he was clearly trying to protect his son with this absurd story. After all, we didn't find a body in the woods. There was no body to find.'

With his feet apart and his fists on his hips, Drew stood silhouetted by the hearth. Its flickering glow illuminated his expression of sardonic triumph.

Victor was impassive. Elizabeth had sought refuge in John's arms. Alice – frozen with horror – dug her nails into Patrick's arm; Patrick himself was as stunned as she. Arthur White, collapsed in his chair, utterly distraught, struggled to respond. His lips moved but did not produce a sound.

I expected Henry to lunge for the inspector, but he did not. My friend was completely calm, his face without expression. He eventually said, 'A brilliant deduction, Inspector. I must remind you, however, that Bob Farr is an American citizen. Three years ago he was in his home country. I'm rather surprised you haven't checked that already.'

Drew turned pale and snapped, 'Then how do you explain the

fact you were seen in two places at once? Explain that!'

Henry inclined his head. 'I am not a policeman. I don't have to explain it.'

Drew gave a predatory smile. 'As I suspected, young man: you are bluffing. Let's move on to the murder of Bob Farr. The extraordinary circumstances surrounding the crime lead us to one possible suspect. Who else but you could have orchestrated such a remarkable murder?

'You are touring America with your friend Bob Farr. Of course your act is not as brilliant as Houdini's, for *you* are using a double.'

Henry flinched. The accusations had apparently left him unmoved, but this contempt for his prowess as a magician struck a nerve.

'In the meantime, you learn that your father is still alive,' Drew continued acerbically, 'and so you must kill him all over again. You return to England with Bob Farr, plotting your revenge. I don't know the details of your plan, but I can explain its basic principle.' He pointed an accusing finger at Henry. 'You wanted your father charged with the murder of his own son. The first step: to kill Bob Farr, who could be easily mistaken for you. Indeed, everybody *did* mistake him – except for Mr White. Second step: to ensure the crime is pinned on your father. This is where things went wrong.

'I don't know what you told your friend Bob to convince him to play along, but it doesn't really matter. A day or two before the murder, you break into Mr Darnley's house under cover of darkness – an easy enough task for two acrobats – and you settle in one of the attic rooms to make your preparations. Nobody knows of your return, and so you take the opportunity to spy on people's comings and goings, to eavesdrop on their conversations… this leads you to discover a highly instructive piece of information: Mr Darnley, your father, and the Latimers are going to attempt to summon a spirit in the haunted room! Mr Latimer will be sealed in the room, and it will be your father's responsibility to check on him every half-hour. You immediately see the possibilities, and devise a Machiavellian plan: get rid of Patrick Latimer, murder Bob, place his corpse in the sealed room. Then, when your father comes knocking on the door and does not receive a reply, he will certainly want to see if anything untoward has occurred. He will open the door, breaking the seal... and find himself confronted with the murdered body of his own son. He will inevitably be arrested for murder, and justice will finally be done.

'So much for the plan, there remains the matter of execution. You need to work it out, and fast. Which you do. But everything does not proceed according to your scheme: when your father receives no answer to his knock, he comes downstairs to fetch the others. The seals are broken in front of several witnesses and so, when the body is discovered, your father cannot be suspected of the crime. Therefore, the murder of Bob Farr takes on a supernatural flavour.

'But let us examine how you achieved this remarkable *tour de force*. It is nine o'clock, everybody is in the drawing room. You are in one of the attic rooms with your friend Bob, and that is when you strike the fatal blow. You head downstairs discreetly, leaving the corpse in the room. When Patrick Latimer approaches the coat rack, you knock him unconscious before joining the others, wearing his coat and hat, with the collar turned up and the brim tilted down to conceal your face. You enter the haunted room, and the door is sealed behind you. Once you are alone in the room, you produce a bottle containing reddish liquid that you drizzle onto the coat, and to which you attach a fake dagger. Let's not forget that you're a professional magician, and this kind of accessory will be very easy to come by! Then you lie face-down with your arms crossed under your body, with one hand sticking out – this is a very important detail – and you wait.

'I can picture you there, lying in wait, listening to your father's footsteps on the stairs, hearing his apprehensive tap on the door, followed by a few moments of silence. The door opens, and there you are, playing dead on the floor with a prop dagger in your back, while in the next room there lies a *real* corpse – that of your friend Bob.'

Drew stopped and produced the little rubber ball from his pocket once again. He studied it complacently before showing it to his audience, declaring, 'That is where this little ball comes into play. But I think some additional clarifications are necessary.'

He picked up the book and tapped it with the flat of his hand before continuing, 'As I told you previously, the entire explanation for the murder can be found in this book.' He flipped through a few pages and then, finding the passage he was looking for, began to read aloud: '"Certain fakirs begin their performance with a dazzling demonstration of their powers: controlling the pulse with the power of the mind. A member of the audience is instructed to take hold of the fakir's wrist, and to confirm that the pulse has entirely stopped." This trick used to cause a sensation, until the day Houdini happened to be in the audience, and suggested that if it was so easy, perhaps the fakir could induce his pulse to speed up and slow down at will? Of course this insidious proposition proved impossible, and the pseudo-fakir was forced to sheepishly withdraw. From then on, the pulse-stopping trick disappeared from the music-hall stage. It became public knowledge that a temporary cessation of the pulse can be achieved by placing a small rubber ball under the armpit. By squeezing the ball under one's arm, it is possible to obstruct the blood flow from the radial artery for several seconds...'

Drew's expression turned grave. He spoke slowly now, to

give his words more weight. 'I'm sure you can see now what happened. How was it determined that the man on the floor was really dead? Mr White took his pulse, and found there was no pulse to take. This is because the so-called corpse had a rubber ball under his armpit. An ordinary rubber ball!

'The rest is easy enough to work out. Terrified, the bystanders all head back downstairs to the drawing room to telephone the police. Nobody thinks to check any of the other attic rooms, and the body is left unattended. The coast is clear, and so the murderer gets to his feet and goes into the other room to fetch Bob's corpse, dragging it into the position he has just vacated. And thus, the illusion is complete.'

Satisfied with his performance, which he no doubt considered a masterful display, Drew stared at us, gauging our reactions. Then he gave the constables a signal, and they approached from their positions either side of the door.

He addressed Henry directly, 'For your own sake, young man, I urge you to confess. I can't make any promises, but I'm sure the judge will take it into account...'

'*Inspector*,' Arthur thundered, getting to his feet, 'you are out of your mind. Not only is your accusation monstrous, but it's based on a false premise. The man whose pulse I took was very definitely dead. His wrist was cold! I was a doctor for several years, and I'm perfectly capable of telling the difference between a living man and a dead one! As for your "psychology", Inspector, you can bet that your superiors will be hearing about it. It is an insult to my family. Now, I must ask you to leave.' He gestured imperiously towards the door.

'Father,' Henry intervened, 'don't lose your temper. He's only doing his job.'

Drew clearly could not believe his ears. He was staring at Henry in bewilderment; his prime suspect was now defending him.

'Inspector,' Henry continued calmly, 'I must congratulate you. It's a brilliant piece of work. And of course I'm familiar with the rubber-ball trick. It had in fact already occurred to me to try it out on my friend James.' He gave me a mischievous wink. 'Yes, Inspector, your hypothesis is both ingenious and original.' He looked Drew straight in the eye. 'And I can tell that you still believe I'm responsible for Bob's death. No, Bob was a great friend. I wouldn't have hurt him for the world. Besides, when he was killed, I was still in the USA, attending a conference of entertainers. There were many people present who knew both Bob and myself, and could tell the difference between us. I'll give you their contact details, and you'll find there are at least twenty who can provide me with an alibi for the evening in question. Furthermore, the next morning I gave a performance for the mayor of—'

'All right,' snapped Drew. 'You can be sure I shall be checking on that.'

With that, Drew – discomfited and desperate not to lose face – bowed curtly and left the room. The two constables who trailed after him were struggling to maintain the fabled 'stiff upper lip'. No doubt it was a thrill to see their superior's unbearable disdain and self-importance unceremoniously curtailed.

5

AN IMPOSSIBLE CRIME

Three days later, Inspector Drew was back at the Whites' to offer his sincerest apologies. Henry was entirely cleared of all suspicion: numerous reliable witnesses had confirmed his alibi. He had not left the United States until the day after the murder. Several passengers from the plane back to England remembered the brilliant card tricks he performed for them.

It was also established that Bob Farr had not been in England at the time of the curious double-sighting of Henry at both Oxford and Paddington Stations. He had been in a hospital bed in Washington, recovering from an appendectomy.

Therefore, the mystery remained. Bob Farr was a decent sort, without family and without much money to his name. There was no conceivable motive for his murder. The investigation revealed that he had come to England – for the first time in his life – a mere week before his death; he then spent four days in a hotel in Oxford. After that, the trail went cold.

It would be inaccurate to say his death had truly affected us – apart from Henry, none of us had known him – yet morale was low all the same. For some, Victor Darnley's house was haunted by a bloodthirsty phantom; for others, a dangerous lunatic was on the prowl. Our village was steeped in fear; at nightfall, we would secure ourselves in our homes, making sure to keep a weapon close at hand.

The Latimers were so disturbed they had announced they

would soon be leaving. Alice was a shadow of herself – one night she had suffered a nervous breakdown, and Patrick had made an emergency call to the doctor.

It was the first Saturday in December, exactly two weeks after Bob Farr's murder. I had invited Henry and John for a drink at my place, since my parents were out for the evening.

'So, John, your better half has let you off the leash for the evening, has she?'

John examined the contents of his glass with a slight smile before answering, 'I am at liberty until nine o'clock. But don't worry, I doubt Elizabeth will come running to fetch me if I miss the curfew.'

We toasted Elizabeth's health, and her remarkable generosity.

The clock struck half-past nine. John studied its face. 'I rather think,' he said with a hint of malice, 'you'll be receiving a telephone call soon.'

Henry smiled. The death of his friend Bob had certainly left its mark on him, but after several days he had begun to pull himself together. He was closer to his old self at last.

'This cognac is excellent,' John declared. 'It's a shame the bottle's running dry...'

I interrupted, 'By the way, Henry, I think it's about time you gave us an explanation...'

The cognac had improved the atmosphere immeasurably. All three of us were cheerful, John was completely at ease away from his fearsome wife, and Henry was almost back to normal. It was time for the truth at last.

'Was it really you I saw at Oxford Station three years ago? And if it was, who did the Latimers see in London? We know it couldn't have been Bob Farr.'

Henry was about to speak as I poured out the remaining

cognac. 'Soon,' he said after a moment's reflection. 'I'll explain everything... soon.'

'Do you have a twin brother?'

'Perhaps Bob did?' John put in, evidently pleased with his deduction.

Henry shook his head with a mocking smile. 'You're nowhere near,' he told us. 'But I'm rather surprised nobody has hit upon the real explanation of this little mystery.'

There was a silence. John lit a cigarette and pondered. '"Little mystery," indeed. There's also the "little mystery" of the footsteps in the attic, in case you've forgotten. And the "little mystery" of who attacked your father. And let's not forget about Bob's death either – a murdered man in a locked room. Hardly worth mentioning, is it?' He paused briefly, then said, 'Henry, I can't be sure, but I think you know who's responsible for these little mysteries. I think you know the name of the killer.'

Henry stared back at John for a long time. His eyes gleamed with a milky brilliance. 'Yes,' he admitted, 'I know who it is.'

'Henry!' cried John. 'You've got to – you've got to tell the police! If you truly know who it is... the killer's still out there, he could strike again!'

Henry took a sip of cognac and ran his tongue over his lips. 'No, I don't think so,' he said quietly.

Henry was a skilled magician, but he wasn't clairvoyant. How could he have predicted the terrible tragedy that would unfold within the hour?

The telephone rang.

'Don't move,' said John, getting to his feet. 'It'll be Elizabeth.' He loped out into the hall to answer.

When he was out of the room, I asked Henry, 'Have the Latimers left yet?'

'Last night, I understand.'

'Curious. They didn't even drop round to say goodbye.'

'Victor came over this morning to let us know. They originally planned to leave today; they spent all day yesterday packing. But when Victor woke up this morning, they were already gone – suitcases, car, and all. Victor was outraged. "Incredible," he said, "they left without a word to me! After I put a roof over their heads!"'

'They must have gone around midnight,' I remarked. 'I had some trouble sleeping, and I think I heard a car engine.'

'So did I,' said Henry.

'It's still strange. Well, I suppose Alice's nerves were on edge... but to run off like that in the middle of the night...'

John returned in triumph. 'Half an hour! It was a tough negotiation, but I've won a half-hour's reprieve.'

'You certainly have a way with the ladies,' I remarked ironically.

John didn't seem to hear me. He came towards us, but paused by the window and drew back the curtain. 'It's stopped snowing, but it's about four inches thick on the ground. What a sight! The moon in a pitch-black sky, and that coat of pristine white snow...'

Henry cleared his throat and waved his glass. 'The snow has a strange effect on me, John. It makes me thirsty.'

Finding our supply of cognac exhausted, we resorted to scotch. I relieved my father's cabinet of an expensive bottle, to the unanimous enthusiasm of my friends. We drank a toast to the snow, and its pristine white coat.

A little later, we found ourselves singing 'Happy Birthday' for no good reason. The clock began to chime, and by the time its tenth peal had fallen silent, the telephone had begun to ring.

'You answer it, Henry. If it's Elizabeth again, tell her there's nobody home.'

Henry nodded, grinning, and left the room.

He reappeared minutes later, his eyes alight.

'Well, who was it?'

'Your fiancée, *Mr* Stevens.'

John turned to me with a grin, then came over to shake my hand. 'Congratulations, James. I had no idea you were—'

'But,' I stammered, 'I'm not…'

'She says she'll be stopping by in a little while,' Henry added cheerfully. 'She says not to worry, but the old man has kept her occupied rather longer than she expected…'

'Good heavens, a married woman!' John exclaimed. 'My word, I hate to think what Betty would make of this…'

Henry was standing by the fire. He seemed totally absorbed in contemplating the flames. I could only see him from the back, but he appeared to be struggling not to laugh.

I must have been utterly sloshed not to realise he was pulling our legs. John suddenly understood and burst out laughing. 'I knew it!'

'Forgive me, James,' said Henry, turning to me. 'It was a wrong number. I couldn't resist the urge to play a little trick on you. You have to admit, it was a good one.' Then he turned back towards the fire.

'James, with a fiancée!' John cackled. 'Too good, Henry. Too, too good.'

'And why,' I protested, *'shouldn't* I have a fiancée?'

'Of course, James, of course,' said John, leaning over to give me a pat on the shoulder – which only annoyed me further.

In the end, though, they had me laughing along with them, and we drank a toast to the health of my non-existent fiancée.

The clock chimed a quarter-past ten.

'Oh, lord,' said John, 'I'd better go.'

'You're only ten minutes from home. She won't eat you. Have another drink, man.'

'No, I'd better not. Thank you for hosting us, James. Cheerio, Henry.'

And John slipped out. Henry stared at the door which had just closed behind him, then smacked his palm with his fist, saying, 'James, what about a game of chess?'

'Excellent idea! It's been over three years since I last gave you a good trouncing.'

'We'll see, we'll see...'

Henry was an impressive opponent, but that evening I was on fine form. The game and the bottle of scotch were finished by quarter to eleven, when I calmly uttered the fateful 'Checkmate.'

Despite his apparent good cheer, I could tell he was as irritated as I was gleeful.

'Rematch?' I suggested casually.

Henry glanced at the empty bottle, then said, 'We appear to have drained your father's drinks cabinet. Why don't you come over to my place?'

'If you think it'll give you a home-field advantage, why not?'

Henry frowned. 'Father may have gone to bed. Do you mind if I use your telephone?'

'Of course.'

Henry went into the hall.

'Strange,' he said on his return.

'No answer?'

'I telephoned several times. At first the line was busy, then it rang normally but nobody answered.'

'That doesn't make sense. Perhaps there's a problem with the line.'

'Perhaps,' said Henry, looking worried.

A shiver ran down my spine. The false good cheer we had enjoyed throughout the evening had finally deserted us.

'Shall we head over there?' I asked. 'After all, I'm waiting for my rematch.'

'Rematch? Ah! Yes, a rematch. All right, let's go.'

Henry's thoughts were obviously elsewhere. He lit a cigarette with a shaky hand. He helped me to clear away the glasses and empty the ashtrays, then we got into our coats.

The clock had just struck eleven when we stepped out of the house. An intense chill took us in its grip. The bright, round moon eclipsed the stars, casting a mantle of white radiance across the landscape. The thick layer of snow cushioned our footsteps.

Henry gazed around, then slowly lifted his head. He grabbed me by the arm and said in a toneless voice, 'James. The moon is red.'

I looked at him closely. His eyes were fixed on the sky.

I shook him gently. 'Henry? What's the matter?'

'Blood-red.'

'What are you talking about? It looks white to me.'

'If you say so. But it frightens me.'

'Frightens you?'

'Yes.' He spoke now with more firmness in his voice. 'It's a full moon. That can have a strange effect on people. On murderers, for instance. I wonder if I was a little hasty when I said the killer wouldn't strike again.'

Our eyes met. The same thought had crossed our minds: Arthur had not answered the telephone.

The crunch of our footsteps in the snow was the only sound that disturbed the silence. I recalled the winters of our happy childhood, when we stepped out into fresh snow with joy in our hearts and studs on our shoes. Those carefree days were long past; once again, evil lurked.

We had almost reached the house when a shadow moved to the left of us. Victor!

'Mr Darnley,' I called out, 'what's the matter? What are you doing out in your pyjamas?'

He had put on an overcoat over his night clothes. There was a dreadful expression on his face, and he spoke in a quivery voice.

'The killer,' he said, indicating the White house. 'He's struck again. Arthur telephoned me a few minutes ago... he's been shot. I think he's very badly wounded. I've telephoned a doctor and the police...'

We dashed the rest of the way over to Arthur's home. When we reached the gate, I turned to my companions. 'We must be careful. The killer might still be in the house. Look – there are no footprints.'

The steps up to the front door were covered in pristine white snow. In fact, we had not seen a single footprint since leaving my place. We were the first ones to walk here since the snow had ceased.

Looking stricken, Henry approached the door and pressed the bell button. Without waiting for an answer, he took a key from his pocket and inserted it into the lock. We entered the hall and Henry turned on the light; our eyes were immediately drawn to the dark stains on the floor.

'Father?' Henry called out.

Silence.

'Stay here, Mr Darnley,' I instructed. 'You never know, the killer might try to get out this way.'

'Right, right,' Victor stammered, looking sick with fear.

Henry made straight for his father's room. I had noticed a sliver of light coming from the drawing room, so I headed that way.

The door was ajar. A small lamp by the window was lit. I turned on the light switch beside the door. By the glow of the chandelier, I examined the room in silence: blood on the floor, on the carpet... I examined the telephone; the receiver had been replaced, and was also covered in blood.

Henry burst into the room. 'There's blood all over the bed... The gun is on the floor... but I can't find Father anywhere! I've looked in all the rooms and...' His voice faded. He pointed towards the armchair, his eyes wide. There was somebody sitting there.

With a lump in my throat, I approached the chair. It was Arthur, slumped sideways in his pyjamas. His left ear was little more than bloody pulp, but his lips... his lips were moving.

'Henry! He's alive!'

'Father, we're here. Please, whatever you do, don't move. We're going to help you, the doctor is on his way.'

It was three in the morning.

Drew sat in a chair by the telephone, looking dejected, smoking one cigarette after another. He ran a hand through his hair, took a deep breath and said, 'Let's go through it again from the beginning. There's not much else we can do for now. Mr Darnley, at around quarter to eleven your neighbour telephoned you. Can you repeat what he said?'

'I believe it was something like "The killer... oh, my head... there was a noise... I woke up... there was a shadow... a gunshot... It hurts, Victor, come quickly. I'm dying. Quickly..."'

'At that very moment,' said Henry in a choked voice, 'I was trying to call my father. Obviously the line was busy. Then I called again, and there was no answer. Oh God, please let him pull through...'

'The scene is easy enough to reconstruct,' said Drew. 'The killer surprises Mr White in his bedroom and shoots him in the head. The bullet catches his ear. We haven't yet compared Mr White's fingerprints to those on the rifle, but I am almost certain the killer placed the weapon in his hands to make it look like suicide. Let's not forget that he used the victim's own weapon to fire the shot.'

'Ever since what happened to Bob Farr,' interrupted Henry, 'Father has kept a loaded rifle by his bedside. The killer must have known that.'

'Who else knew it?' Drew asked sharply.

'I'd rather not say,' Henry averred. 'I wouldn't want you to think I was accusing anybody…'

'I knew about it,' declared Victor Darnley.

'Me too,' I admitted. 'But we weren't the only ones. There's my parents, my sister, John, the Latimers, and several others.'

'In any case, that leaves us with a limited list of suspects,' said Drew. 'So, after committing his crime, the murderer flees the scene…'

'But, Inspector,' I said, 'that's impossible. There were no footprints…'

Faced with a dark look from Drew, I fell silent.

'But Mr White is not dead,' he continued. 'In spite of his terrible injury, he manages to reach the drawing room and to telephone you, Mr Darnley. This is at a quarter to eleven. Finally, he collapses in the armchair. Yes, it must have happened that way. The trail of blood helps us to retrace his steps.' Drew paused. 'That is all clear. But there remains one unexplained detail: where did the killer go? We've searched the whole house twice: nothing. We know that it stopped snowing at nine o'clock and that Mr White's injury occurred after that time – the doctor was quite clear on the point. However, there are no footprints in the snow anywhere around the house – except for yours near the front door, of course.'

'The back door was ajar,' Henry pointed out. 'It leads into the garden.'

'So what?' said Drew. 'You know as well as I do, there wasn't a single footprint out there either. But my men aren't finished yet; they went to fetch some powerful torches, so perhaps…'

At that moment a policeman entered the room. 'Nothing, Inspector. Nothing at all. I can't understand it. Apart from the footprints left by these gentlemen and by us, there's nothing there. Only smooth white snow. Nothing on the ground, nothing on the window sills or the roof… I think we'd better call off the search.'

'No,' barked Drew. 'That's out of the question. I want you to search the whole house again from top to bottom. The killer must be hiding somewhere.'

The policeman nodded, then left. The inspector's thin lips curled into an evil grin. 'Believe me, when I get my hands on this fellow, he'll be lucky if he makes it to the gallows. Because I *will* catch him, you can be sure of that. I've never failed, and I don't plan to start now.'

'I don't think I'd be so confident in your shoes,' said Victor. 'Everything points towards a supernatural explanation. The American killed in a sealed room, and now the criminal manages to escape without leaving a single print in the snow, as though he can simply float above the ground.

'Spirits do exist, you know. People tend to look at me pityingly when I say that, and I've no doubt they laugh at me behind my back. Except for Arthur and the Latimers, that is…'

'The same Latimers who left last night,' I observed.

'And without a word of farewell,' lamented Victor. 'That's very strange. We were close, you know. They always treated me as a friend…'

Drew's eyebrows rose in astonishment. 'The Latimers are gone? What do you mean, gone? Where have they gone?'

'I've no idea,' said Victor wearily.

'Why did they leave?'

'Since the American died, Alice Latimer hasn't been the same. She suffered a number of nervous breakdowns; I think she was afraid. So they decided to move out. Their departure was planned for today. Yesterday, that is,' he added, looking at the clock. 'But they actually left the evening before, without a word to any of us.'

'How strange,' said Drew, narrowing his eyes. 'So strange, in fact, that I'm going to alert my colleagues. But, in my opinion, they won't have got far. I'm tempted to say that one of them was in this very room only a few hours ago...'

Drew reached for the telephone, but before he grasped it, it started to ring of its own accord. He took a moment to collect himself, then answered.

'Drew here.'

As the seconds ticked past, his expression grew more grave. After hanging up, he lit a cigarette and took a few anxious puffs, blowing them out through his nostrils. He rubbed his forehead, then informed us, 'Mr White is dead. If we'd been here half an hour earlier, we might have saved him. He would have had life-changing aftereffects, but we'd have saved him.'

Henry left the room, his head in his hands. Victor followed.

There was a silence. Drew stubbed out his cigarette.

'This is terrible,' he said to me, obviously troubled. 'To think I accused your friend of plotting against his father, and now his father is dead. I was foolish to look for similarities between his personality and Houdini's. All the character studies and psychology did was lead me to a false conclusion. I admit, young man, I'm not very proud of myself at the moment.'

This was quite an admission, and clearly hadn't come easily. I felt rather sorry for him.

'The doctor,' he continued, 'confirmed the shot couldn't have been fired before nine forty-five or after ten-thirty. The bullet was lodged in the skull, just behind the left ear – which it tore off en route. If we'd got here earlier, he might have had a chance. But all this damned snow slowed everything down. Still,' his sorrowful expression was slowly replaced by that familiar thin, sardonic smile, 'the killer is still out there – but not for long.'

He picked up the telephone and dialled a number, before wishing me a good night. Taking this as a dismissal, I left the room. But just as I was pulling the door shut behind me, I heard his voice.

'Put out an alert. "Wanted by police: Alice and Patrick Latimer."'

6

WHODUNIT?

Victor must have alerted my parents – they were waiting for me when I got home. I had expected them to bombard me with questions, but they were too distraught. I retreated to bed, seeking refuge under the covers, but there was no peace or quiet to be had. Instead, the full extent of the absurdity and horror of these recent events unravelled in my mind. First, the murder of Bob Farr, and now Arthur White. They had nothing in common; there was no connection between the two men – except for Henry. The same Henry who was going to be a very wealthy young man now that his father was dead. But he could not have killed either of the men; he was in America when Bob Farr was killed, and his father had been shot at around ten o'clock, when his alibi was supplied by John and myself. It was quite impossible.

John had left us at ten-fifteen… could it have been him? No, impossible. Not John. Besides, he had no motive. Unless – perhaps his long-standing jealousy of Henry? Henry was the obvious suspect in both cases – I couldn't help but wonder if the whole mess was a convoluted scheme to send him to the gallows.

Let's consider everyone who lacked an alibi for both crimes. First, John. Then… Elizabeth? I saw no reason to exclude her from my list of suspects. And what of Patrick? Patrick, who had vanished without trace? The Latimers' hasty departure under cover of darkness was curious, to say the least. Besides, Drew had made his suspicions plain by issuing that 'wanted' notice at half-past three in the morning. But the criminal might have operated with an accomplice. This meant that neither Henry, Alice, nor Victor ought to be ruled out. Alas, this possibility shed no light on exactly *how* the murders were committed; our devilish killer still seemed to possess the ability to walk through walls or fly through the air. The whole thing was absurd, utterly absurd.

Where had it all started? With Mrs Darnley's singular suicide? With the sound of the phantom footsteps? With Mrs White's message from beyond the grave?

There was another point which remained a mystery: nobody had heard the shot that killed Arthur. Victor was in a deep sleep at the time – that much was understandable – but John, Henry and I ought to have heard something. We were tipsy, of course – but not as tipsy as all that!

All these questions jostled for my attention; they tangled and untangled themselves in my poor head. Any attempt to gather my thoughts was in vain; the only explanations I could come up with were completely irrational.

Then, sleep finally washed over me in an insidious wave.

A funeral procession is moving slowly towards the churchyard, accompanied by the mournful monotony of the resounding bell. Four men dressed in black and pale of face bear the coffin on their shoulders. Behind them trail the mourners. I recognise Henry, Victor, John, Elizabeth, Patrick, Alice, and myself. The sky overhead is choked with crows, swirling above that sad parade. Suddenly, and for no apparent reason, the birds begin to panic; the beating of their wings grows agitated, their crowing becomes shrill and their movements frantic.

A dark creature begins to descend from the clouds. Bird of prey? Phantom? It is a woman dressed in shapeless rags, her eyes aglow with hatred. She hovers for a moment before advancing on our mournful procession, arm upraised, accusatory index finger pointing to one person among us…

*

The next day, Father woke me just before noon to let me know my friend had arrived. I had a quick wash – which helped to remove the scent of alcohol, at least, and the remaining vestiges of my nightmare. But the reality it left behind was hardly much better. Then I went down to the drawing room.

Henry was sitting in an armchair. He got up and came over to meet me; we exchanged a silent handshake. His dark clothing made him look pale, but there was a sad serenity in his eyes. He was no longer the little boy who had mourned his mother's death for weeks on end; now he was a man who faced his misfortune with grace and dignity.

I was all he had left now. His lifelong friend, who was more like a brother to him. We had known each other all our lives; we had gone to school together, played games together, eaten together, got up to all kinds of mischief together. Now I was all the family he had left – I could read as much in his face.

Father cleared his throat, no doubt to conceal his emotion, then declared, 'Henry is going to spend a few days with us, James. He'll be staying in Elizabeth's old room. We just need to move those boxes of clothes she doesn't wear any more. I've told her time and again to come and collect them.'

I nodded.

Father continued, 'Care for some brandy, gentlemen? No answer? I'll take that as a "yes", shall I?'

He went over to the cabinet. 'Heavens above! The bottle's empty. Then it had better be scotch – wait a moment, that's all gone too.'

Henry looked at me with a slight smile. He opened his mouth to say something, but I made a gesture for him to keep quiet.

Father went on, 'My darling wife has taken to hiding liquor bottles occasionally, she says she does it for my health. But if she's started pouring the stuff away – well, that's quite intolerable.

A flagrant abuse of power. I'm going to give her a piece of my mind.'

He left the room in as dignified a manner as he could manage.

'Don't move,' I whispered to Henry. Then I dashed up to my room to fetch a bottle of whisky I always kept in reserve.

'James!' Henry exclaimed. 'Surely you're not going to—?'

'I am,' I said, heading for the drinks cabinet. I refilled the two bottles we had emptied last night, and just had time to sit down beside Henry, tucking the empty bottle behind my back.

At that moment, Father returned to the room with Mother in tow. She looked utterly bewildered. He flung open the doors to the cabinet and glared at her.

'Who has emptied the cognac and whisky away?'

Perplexed, Mother looked at the bottles, then glared at her husband.

'Edward,' she announced, 'I think you had better get to an optician.'

I watched Henry from the corner of my eye; he was struggling not to laugh. My mission was accomplished.

'An optician?' replied Father, horrified. 'I, a Stevens, consult an optician? Nobody in this family has ever needed or worn spectacles. Even my grandfather, who lived to be ninety-eight. Why on earth should I see an optician? Nothing wrong with my eyes, is there?'

Without a word, Mother took the two bottles from the cabinet and brandished them under his nose. Father grabbed them and examined them incredulously.

Mother turned on her heel and spoke over her shoulder. 'Lunch is ready when you are.' As she left the room she glanced once more at her husband, who was lost in contemplation of the two bottles.

Throughout the meal, during which Father struggled to keep the conversation going, Henry was quiet. By the time we were having coffee, though, he was his loquacious self again – thanks to Father, who happened to mention an uncle of his who had known Houdini.

'Your uncle knew Houdini?' repeated Henry in amazement.

Father examined the ceiling in thoughtful silence, savouring the rich smoke from his cigar. 'Richard,' he eventually said, 'was a journalist. He emigrated to America, and worked for a newspaper in Chicago – I forget the name, it was such a long time ago.

'Anyway, Houdini had just performed one of his famous escapes, and Richard went to write an article about it. After that, the two of them became quite friendly.'

Mother and I stared at him in disbelief. He had never mentioned this Uncle Richard before; I strongly suspected he had invented him with the sole aim of keeping Henry amused.

'When Richard came back to England,' Father continued, visibly satisfied with the reaction his story had received, 'he often talked about Houdini. Houdini the Magnificent! Houdini, King of Escapologists!'

Henry was lapping all this up.

'What's more,' Father went on with a dreamy smile, 'my uncle had a wonderful sense of humour. There was one particular story he liked to tell, and it would make us weep with laughter. Houdini had been invited to a dog show, and he asked my uncle to accompany him. So they went along, and were greeted by a group of middle-aged women who couldn't wait to show off their little doggies.'

I was now quite sure he was making it up; this was just the sort of story he liked to tell.

'At the end of the evening, there was a film screening. You can guess what it was about. The dogs were placed in another room, with a cage for each of them. No sooner had the film started rolling than the guests heard a heartbreaking sound from the other room — but it wasn't the dogs, in fact it was *meowing*. I'll spare you the description of all those ladies dolled up in their finery, dashing for the door. It was like a henhouse where a puma has just got loose!'

Mother, who was no longer interested in her husband's tall tales, got up from the table.

'Could you bring in the cognac, my dear?' Father asked delicately. Then, returning his attention to Henry and me, he went on, 'You can imagine their amazement when they found that each cage now contained a *cat* instead of their beloved canines! There was much fainting; ambulances were called.

'Richard never knew how Houdini had accomplished this incredible substitution — the two men had not been apart at all during the evening.'

'Then he must have had an accomplice,' Henry suggested.

'An accomplice,' repeated Father thoughtfully. 'Roughly forty dogs had been replaced by the same number of cats in the space of ten minutes. I don't see how he might have—'

Mother reappeared, placing three glasses and the infamous bottle of cognac on the table. Father did the honours, then continued with his tale, 'But that's not all! A short while later,' he took a little sip, 'there was another miracle: the dogs were back in their cages, and the cats were gone — every last one of them. It's incredible, but it's true. Houdini had managed to swap them all back again…'

Father's voice died away. He frowned. Then he picked up his glass again and emptied it in a single gulp. For a moment, I thought his eyes were going to pop out of his head.

'Darling,' he stammered, 'I think you may be right. You'd better call a doctor — I'm losing my marbles. First my eyesight is going, now I can't tell the difference between cognac and whisky!'

*

That afternoon, Henry and I went for a walk in the country. We moved peacefully across that vast, dazzling, snowy expanse. Though the sun was bright, a sharp chill nipped at our faces.

'James,' said Henry after a silence, 'you shouldn't have played that trick on your father. Especially since we were the ones who drank all his cognac.'

'He was asking for it.'

Henry smiled at me. 'The switch from cognac to whisky was a trick... but I doubt the metamorphosis of dogs into cats ever existed outside of your father's imagination.'

'You know what he's like,' I said. 'He may well have met a journalist who rubbed shoulders with Houdini, but I've certainly never heard of an "Uncle Richard".' I had to admit, though, that Father's plan had worked; he had succeeded in distracting Henry, which was his main aim.

'Houdini...' said Henry dreamily. 'What a remarkable fellow. Truly, a dazzling phenomenon. You know, James, that book the inspector was showing us the other day – I've read it time and time again...'

'By the way, you don't blame him for trying to pin the murder on you, do you?'

'No,' Henry answered categorically. 'The man was just doing his job. He's very intelligent, by the way. *Very* intelligent. His explanation for the locked-room murder was remarkable. True, he didn't have all the available data, but still, he wasn't far from the truth...'

'Henry!' I exclaimed in horror. 'You don't mean to say that you—'

'No, of course not. But I know how it was done, thanks to you.'

'To me?'

'Thanks to your account of what happened. Do you remember

the strange feeling you experienced when you went up to that attic the second time?'

'A strange feeling... yes, I remember it, but I can't quite put my finger on it.'

'Your eyes were taking everything in, but your mind couldn't quite process it.'

'Henry,' I said, 'don't you think it's about time you told the police the name of your suspect? This is the monster who killed your father, after all. Staying silent might even be a criminal act, particularly if it continues to prolong this nightmare...'

He looked at me seriously. 'I suppose you're aware that the killer is a member of our tight-knit little circle?'

A chill ran down my spine. In my mind's eye I saw a parade of faces: John, Elizabeth, Victor, Alice, Patrick... One of them was a murderer. No; it couldn't be John. Nor Elizabeth. Nor Victor! That left the Latimers.

'Henry,' I said, 'Drew strongly suspects the Latimers of murdering your father.'

My friend's only answer was a shake of the head and a heavy sigh.

We didn't say much to one another on our return journey to the village, but Henry did broach the subject of 'proportion"

'Proportion?' I repeated. 'What do you mean, proportion?'

'Yes, proportion,' he said with a sparkle of mischief in his eyes. 'That's what gave you such a strange feeling. Proportion.'

The cogs in my brain had ceased to function. His words seemed to make no sense. I now looked at Henry not with pity but with frustration; I would quite gladly have throttled him on the spot.

During the afternoon, policemen continued to search in and around the Darnley house. Drew, evidently irritated by their lack of progress, had clearly instructed them to leave no stone unturned.

I heard one of them swearing behind the house, and then Drew raged: 'On your feet, man! What did I do to deserve such cretins?'

'Sorry, sir. I caught my foot in something. Couldn't see it because of the snow. It looks like some sort of spring.'

'And what do you want *me* to do about it?'

'Charming as ever, our dear inspector,' Henry observed mockingly.

We overheard Victor offering tea to warm the chilly bones of the investigators. Drew permitted it, 'for the sake of morale', he claimed, all the while bemoaning the time wasted — though clearly not averse to a bit of respite from the cold.

Supper time passed in a strange silence. I was still irritated with Henry for refusing to reveal the solution to the mystery, which he claimed to possess. I could never have imagined that this very evening, this drab Sunday in December, the whole sinister story was fast approaching its finale — and what an unimaginably grim finale it would prove to be.

I sat staring at the food on my plate, pondering all the while what Henry had meant by that curious word, 'proportion'. Father was not his usual talkative self; he kept his head down, eating quietly. Feeling sorry for him, I told him how the cognac had disappeared and then transformed into whisky. This caused him to sit upright, glaring at me. Henry struggled to contain his mirth, while Mother burst out laughing. If there's one thing Father cannot stand, it's his wife making fun of him.

'You shouldn't have done that, son,' he said solemnly, before leaving the room with his head held high.

'He'll be in a mood for the rest of the week,' said Mother when she had regained her composure. It then became apparent to her that all this hilarity was misplaced in the aftermath of the recent tragedy. 'Forgive me, Henry,' she said gently. 'I couldn't help myself.'

'Mrs Stevens,' said Henry, 'I haven't thanked you properly yet for your most generous invitation. Ever since Mother's death…' His voice grew choked; his expression darkened.

That was when the telephone began to ring. A moment later, the door creaked open a little and Father grunted, 'James, it's for you.'

I went out into the hall just in time to see him disappearing into the drawing room. He was clearly more upset than I had thought.

The receiver lay beside the telephone. I grabbed it and blurted, 'What's the matter, Elizabeth?'

A voice that was clearly not Elizabeth answered drily, 'Drew here.'

'Oh! Inspector, I…'

'Can you come round, young man? You and your friend?'

'Of course, where to?'

'Next door, to Mr Darnley's. Your sister and brother-in-law are already here.'

'I see. What's this all about?'

'I have reason to believe that… Well, you'd better come round. I'll explain everything then.'

'Very well. We're on our way.'

'And one last piece of advice, young man: *be careful*. I know who the killer is, but he's still on the loose. So *be careful*.'

'All right,' I said, catching a frightening glimpse of my stricken-looking features in the mirror above the telephone.

Five minutes later, Henry and I were traipsing over to Victor's house. It was dark by now; the pale halo of light from the street lamp was dimmed by flurries of snow.

The imposing silhouette of the house loomed above us, its towering gables capped with snow. With a shudder, I pushed open the front gate. We walked the hedge-lined path towards the stone steps.

Victor answered the door. 'Come in, let me take your coats. The others are in the drawing room – the *upstairs* drawing room, that is.'

We stepped into the hall. As he relieved us of our coats, Victor's blue eyes took in Henry with a melancholy gaze.

Henry gave a sigh. 'I'm all right, Mr Darnley. Or rather, I will be.' He went up the stairs and I followed. We entered the drawing room, where a fire crackled in the hearth, filling the place with a pleasant warmth. But the room itself gave me quite a shock – so morbid! Where the hell had Alice found that wallpaper? It looked for all the world like the black silk favoured by high-end tailors.

Opposite the door was a large sofa of dazzling red velvet. To the right was the fireplace and an armchair of that same velvet. There were two windows in the far wall, but one of them was now covered. To the left of the door was a small wooden chest with a strange silver-clasped *grimoire* propped on top of it. Beside this was a pedestal table covered by a black velvet cloth with silver edges, and on top of that stood the crystal ball. Several chairs were arranged around the table, and the room was decorated with thick, black curtains held in place by silver-tasselled cords. The whole place resembled a funeral parlour.

Milky light issued from a round, opaline ceiling fixture and several wall lamps resembling *torchères*. Their dingy glow, combined with the blood-red carpet underfoot, gave the room a strange ambiance.

To cap it all, the other window behind the sofa was now boarded up with a large midnight-blue wooden panel – most likely Patrick's handiwork – on which was painted a baleful moon and enigmatic drifting shadows, which seemed to reach out like imploring hands. And then there were the two faux-marble pillars which flanked the crystal ball on either side. It was a triumph of bad taste.

How on earth could rational human beings be taken in by this ridiculous backdrop? It was perhaps more understandable for Victor, whose grief had dulled all other senses. But Mr White?

Elizabeth sat on the sofa, snuggling close to John. Drew was in his usual position, leaning against the mantel, with a cigarette drooping from the corner of his mouth.

'At last you're here,' he snapped. 'What's this, Mr Stevens? You seem rather perturbed by the look of the place.'

'Indeed I am,' I confessed.

Drew addressed Victor, who had just followed us into the room. 'This is where the séances took place, isn't that right?'

'Please don't mock things you do not understand, Inspector,' Victor responded softly. 'The Latimers left in a hurry, I'll admit. But that's no reason to accuse them of murder.'

'A hurry,' Drew sneered, 'is an understatement. Apart from a few personal effects, they left everything behind. My men have spent a good part of the afternoon searching the rooms they used to occupy, and found many valuable items simply abandoned. And that's without even mentioning the clothes; the suits and the dresses… No, they did not "leave in a hurry", Mr Darnley, they *fled*.'

Drew paused, and I took the opportunity to sit down on the sofa next to John. I grimaced; it was remarkably uncomfortable. Patrick seemed to have replaced the upholstery with three large cushions, draped a velvet cloth over them and tacked a wooden board to the base to hold the entire thing together. I pointed this out to Elizabeth, who said, 'All style and no substance – just like them.'

Drew silenced us with a look, then continued, 'It has been two days since the Latimers went missing, and for the last twenty-four hours police all over the country have been looking for them. For the moment, though, they remain at large. But they will be found, mark my words. However, it's important to note that during the three years since they moved in here, their bank balance has grown considerably. I believe I know the source of their income: Mrs Alice Latimer charges dearly for her services as a so-called medium. And she had plenty of clients, isn't that so, M. Darnley?'

'"So-called medium"!' Victor fumed. 'How dare you, Inspector? Mrs Latimer has a real gift. If you'd attended one of her séances you would have seen it for yourself. It's only natural for her to share her gifts with others—'

'For a price,' retorted Drew. 'The Latimers started exploiting people long before they came here. But they did it under another name, which is why it's taken a while to prove. I received the details just this morning.'

'You mean to say they are frauds?' said Elizabeth, clearly taken aback.

'Precisely.'

'My God! Patrick was always so pleasant, so charming!'

John gave her a look, then mimicked, 'My God! Alice was always so beautiful…'

'Oh, shut up,' Elizabeth interrupted. 'I'm getting tired of your jealousy.'

John was duly abashed.

'If I understand correctly,' said Henry, 'you are also under the impression that they are murderers?'

'Yes,' Drew replied. 'They are responsible for the deaths of both your friend and your father. Their sudden flight is tantamount to a confession.'

'But why?' I said. 'And how?'

Drew's thin lips curled into that mocking smile of his. 'Why? Well, it's easy enough to imagine the victims uncovering their shenanigans. As for how, I can't be sure just yet. But they'll make a full confession when I catch them, just you wait.

'For now, I will share with you my theory concerning Mr

White's murder. Here's what we know: the crime took place at around ten o'clock. It had stopped snowing an hour earlier, and there are no footprints anywhere near the house – except for those of the people who discovered the victim, of course. And the murderer had completely vanished by the time we arrived. Therefore the murderer, as impossible as it may seem, had escaped from the house without leaving a trace.

'I remind you that the back door, which leads to the rear garden, was open. Roughly five yards away from the door is a fruit tree. Behind that is another, then another, and so on. A system of ropes strung between the trees in advance would have enabled the killer to get away without leaving a trace. And a few special knots would allow him to untie them with a simple tug...'

'Ingenious,' said Henry with a smile. 'But wouldn't the ropes have left a mark when they dropped to the ground?'

'The killer might have used a long stick to keep them in place,' Drew murmured. 'I don't know, it's just a theory. You're the acrobat – what do you think?'

'Quite honestly, I don't buy it,' said Henry. 'It would require sophisticated equipment and specialist knowledge. Even then, it would have been impossible to rig all this up without anybody noticing; Father and I were at home all afternoon, you know. And there's something else – the killer had no way of knowing when the snow was going to stop falling. Or even if it was going to snow at all. So it would be a bit, shall we say, risky?'

'I think you're right, young man,' Drew admitted regretfully.

There was a silence.

The Latimers' guilt was far from certain. They might conceivably have had a motive for murdering Arthur White; perhaps he had discovered some incriminating information. But why kill Bob Farr, a man they didn't know existed?

The inspector was wrong. The killer was in this very room.

Elizabeth broke the silence. 'John, your hand is freezing.'

'What are you talking about, darling?'

Drew paced thoughtfully back and forth in front of the fireplace. He threw his cigarette into the fire, then cleared his throat to draw our attention.

'We know who's responsible. We know they are on the run. But where would they go? Perhaps not as far away as we thought. The reason I gathered you here this evening is to issue a warning: our suspects are at large, and very dangerous. They won't hesitate to take another life. You must all be very careful.

'*But*,' he added with a glint in his eye, 'we're closing in. And when I lay my hands on them, they'll wish they'd never been born. In fact, they'll be lucky to get out alive.'

You'll have to catch them first, I thought. The sofa was now unbearable; the stuffing had completely gone out of it.

'John, you're so cold! Your hand is frozen.'

John got to his feet and stood facing his wife. 'What are you talking about? How do you know if my hand is cold or not?'

Drew was paying no attention to John and Elizabeth. Gazing down at his clenched fist with a threatening smile, he repeated, 'They'll be lucky to get out alive.'

John held up both hands so my sister could see them. Elizabeth was now very still, and all the colour had vanished from her face. She spoke in a scarcely audible voice, 'Your hand is frozen…'

John staggered back in horror. I stood, and saw what had startled him. Elizabeth was holding onto another hand; one which protruded between the sofa cushions and the backrest.

She collapsed in a faint; I caught her and whisked her away from the sofa. Drew hurled the cushions across the room.

The killer had struck again. The sofa had been gutted of its springs; in their place lay the bodies of Alice and Patrick Latimer.

This made no sense at all. It was a living nightmare. My head started to spin. All the same, I was quite certain – irrationally certain, perhaps, but certain nonetheless – that the killer was in this very room. It was a small circle of suspects; they could be counted on the fingers of one hand.

One, Henry. Two, Elizabeth. Three, John. Four, Victor. Five… Inspector Drew. After all, why not?

PART THREE

ENTR'ACTE

There! Finished.

And what a story! If Dr Twist can untangle *this* little mess I shall take my hat off to him.

Before I go on, let me introduce myself. My name is Ronald Bowers, and I write detective fiction under the pseudonym 'John Carter'. It's 1979 and I am approximately fifty years old. I say 'approximately' because I cannot be entirely sure of my age... but that's another story.

What you have just read is fiction. James Stevens, Henry White, Alice Latimer, and all the others were created barely two weeks ago for the purpose of a bet with Dr Twist. (I won't insult your intelligence by introducing Alan Twist, that great criminologist who has solved countless remarkable mysteries in a long, illustrious career.)

He's not a young man any more, but remains as sharp as ever. His passion for gardening keeps him in shape, though he doesn't get out much these days. His grey matter is entirely intact, and he frequently gives Scotland Yard the benefit of his advice.

A fortnight ago, he invited me to spend the evening at his place. Whenever we meet, there is only one topic that dominates our conversation: crime. Naturally, that evening was no exception.

'My dear Ronald,' he said to me, 'I'm going to tell you a secret. I've spent my life catching some of the cleverest, most diabolical murderers, and solving the most baffling mysteries. But there's one thing in the field of crime that I've never managed to accomplish.'

'And what's that?'

'To write a mystery novel. To create a flawless puzzle. I think I'm right in saying I have a knack for solving mysteries. But contriving them from scratch? No. I've tried several times, but never managed to pull it off.'

'Doctor, I can hardly believe it. Writing mysteries is easy. The difficult part is solving them. Trust me, I know whereof I speak. I think you're pulling my leg. With all the experiences you've had, surely it would be easy to…'

'To explain the impossible, yes. But not to write a story, to create characters, a setting… I've tried again and again, and I simply cannot do it.'

'All right, Doctor. What of it?'

'That, my dear Ronald, is why I am calling upon the services of the greatest living mystery writer: Ronald Bowers, alias John Carter.'

'Thank you for the compliment, Doctor, but you give me too much credit. There are plenty of others who—'

'No. You are undoubtedly the best. The only one who writes mysteries worthy of the name. Your contemporaries have let gratuitous sex and violence creep into their work in place of the plot. You, however, are the last living exponent of the authentic fair-play mystery.'

'Thank you, Doctor, but let's not get carried away. What is it you're after, exactly?'

'I'd like us to collaborate. You will handle the atmosphere, the characters, the plot – a baffling tale of ghosts and locked-room murders, do you see?'

'I do.'

'A dazzling, remarkable mystery – and you won't need to worry about the solution, because that's *my* job!'

'It's a tempting idea, I'll admit. But unfortunately it's impossible. The author needs to know the solution to the mystery before he can start writing. Of course I *could* write a bizarre mystery story without a rational explanation, but there's no way you'd be able to solve it. It would be impossible. I know I'm repeating myself, but it's vital to know the solution before…'

'Yes or no, my dear Ronald. Will you give it a try?'

'All right, but I've no intention of going easy on you. I guarantee you won't be able to come up with a satisfactory solution. You've been warned!'

'We shall see. We shall see.'

That's why I wrote this remarkable story. I must admit, I've had a blast! To write an utterly fantastic mystery without worrying about the solution – what a treat! And so wonderfully easy. The preceding pages came to me with scarcely any effort at all, practically all at once, over the course of ten evenings. I let myself get a little tipsy, which I don't normally do when I'm writing.

Another innovation: I've written it in the first person. My protagonist, James Stevens, is also the narrator; that's something I've never done before. I hope Twist doesn't make poor James the murderer! He's certainly capable of it!

No, James couldn't be the killer. He has an unshakeable alibi for both murders. The Latimers would have made likely suspects; naturally, I thought of that. It's why I had to kill them off in the last few pages, so Dr Twist couldn't fall back on that hypothesis.

It might even be the reincarnation of Houdini – master of mystery, such a perfect foil for a detective story! – in the person of young Henry White. Perhaps Henry held his father responsible for his mother's death, and so began to hatch his bloodthirsty scheme. But I've ruled this out too.

Poor Dr Twist, there's simply no way round it. Well, he can't say I didn't warn him.

I shall send him the manuscript tomorrow. What time is it now? Three o'clock in the morning! I must have been typing for eight hours straight! This story has absorbed me so completely, it's almost as if—

The telephone breaks my train of thought. At this hour, it could only be Jimmy.

'Hello?'

'Hello, Ronald. Not waking you, am I?'

'Perhaps you should have asked yourself that question before dialling? As a matter of fact, no. I was writing.'

'I've got a fantastic idea, absolutely brilliant! That's why I simply had to call you. You can use it in your next novel.'

'I'm listening.'

'A man is seen getting into an old suit of armour – in front of witnesses, of course. After a minute or two, he stops moving and everyone starts to get worried. Perhaps he's ill or something, you know? So they go to check on him. Guess what happens next.'

'The man has disappeared.'

'No. Much better than that: he's still in the armour, but he's completely lost his head.'

'I see. So it's a suit of armour that drives the wearer insane?'

'No, no, he's *really* lost his head. His head has been cut off, and completely vanished! Good one, eh?'

'Very original. And how was it done?'

'That's for you to work out – but I'm sure you can do it! It's a nice idea though, isn't it?'

'Well, it certainly bears some thinking about. Now, if there's nothing else, I'd like to get some sleep. I'll see you tomorrow, lunch time, at the White Horse?'

'Certainly, certainly. I'm sure you'll be able to do something with my idea. It could be an old manor house, where the squire is a descendant of Bluebeard...'

'Tell me tomorrow, Jimmy. Good night.'

I hang up and breathe a long sigh.

He's a decent sort, that Jimmy, but he can be a real pain sometimes. Used to be a playwright, until he hit the bottle a bit too hard. Fiftyish, like me. Now he's out of work and his wife has left him – truthfully, I feel sorry for him. That's why I let him come up with plot ideas from time to time, and occasionally give him a bit of money for them. I thought it might help him to rebuild his self-esteem.

Anyway, ever since then he's been bombarding me non-stop with his 'great ideas'. I've even used a couple of them as sub-plots, so as not to disappoint him. It's pretty much all they are good for, however; they're just too far-fetched, too improbable... rather like this mystery without a solution which I'm sending to Dr Twist.

In fact, now that I think of it, I can't help but wonder if one of Jimmy's ideas might have crept into the story I've just finished. Subconsciously, I mean. It's not impossible; after all, I wrote the story so quickly, almost as if it were writing itself...

Damn that Jimmy! From now on, I'd better write down all his ideas, otherwise I'll get them mixed up.

Quarter past three. Well past your bedtime, Ronald old chap!

Jimmy stood silhouetted in the French window. He was watching the gardener, who was meticulously pruning the rose bushes just outside. Then he ran a hand through his curly hair and turned to face me.

'By the way, Ronald, have you had any thoughts about the decapitated man in the suit of armour? I phoned you about him a couple of weeks ago, at about three in the morning. Do you remember?'

A couple of weeks! It had been two weeks since I sent my manuscript to Dr Twist, and still no response. Not that there was any rush, of course. Even a genius like Twist could not be expected to explain the inexplicable.

'Yes,' I replied, my tone obviously betraying my lack of interest. 'I thought about it, but I didn't get very far.'

Jimmy came over and grabbed a book from my desk. '*Houdini and His Legend*, by Roland Lacourbe,' he said, leafing through the pages. 'Quite a fellow, that Houdini. Have you read this?'

I studied my friend's cheerful, round face, framed by silver curls. He looked concerned.

'If I'm being a nuisance,' he said suddenly, 'all you have to do is tell me and I'll—'

'Not at all! The very idea. Why don't you pour us a drink?'

Jimmy, who had obviously been waiting for this invitation, did so without a word. With a trembling hand he placed a glass on my desk, then emptied his own in one go.

'Ronald,' he said, 'I'd hate to think of myself as some kind of sponger or something. You don't seem all that interested in my ideas any more, and—'

'What are you talking about? You know full well that without you and your ideas "John Carter" would have ceased to exist long ago. And I've often wondered where you get them from. You seem to produce them from thin air, like a magician.'

'True,' said Jimmy modestly, pouring himself another drink.

This little scene was a fairly regular occurrence. Jimmy needed a great deal of reassurance, otherwise he fell to pieces.

'By the way,' I said in a casual manner, 'didn't you mention an idea about Houdini a few months ago?'

'No,' he said firmly.

'Are you sure about that?'

Jimmy looked at me strangely. 'I've never mentioned Houdini, Ronald. He *would* make a good subject, though. I'll have a think about it.' He turned back towards the French window. 'There's the postman. I'll go and fetch the post.'

He went out, then reappeared almost immediately.

'Here you are,' he said, dropping a few envelopes on the desk. 'I'll leave you to it. I'm going out for some air.'

One envelope was larger than the rest. Was it…? Dr Twist!

I wrenched it open; it contained roughly ten typewritten sheets, and a handwritten covering note:

Dear Ronald,

Here is the solution to your mystery. I picked up right where you left off — that is, just after the discovery of Patrick and Alice's bodies. I have continued writing it in the first person as well. The solution came fairly quickly — there could be only one explanation, after all. I admit that I had the benefit of some outside assistance, not in solving the mystery but in writing the epilogue.

I shall say no more for the moment. We can discuss everything at our next meeting.

Yours ever, etc…

The solution 'came fairly quickly'. Well, I never. Had Dr Twist really achieved the impossible? Had he found a path out of my labyrinth of mysteries?

Only one way to find out.

PART FOUR

1
EXPLANATIONS

My head was spinning. John escorted Elizabeth away, and Victor's voice broke the chilly silence of that charnel house.

'It was the only possible explanation… Patrick and Alice would never have left without saying goodbye. You said it yourself, Inspector: they would have been lucky to get out alive.'

Drew was utterly dumbfounded, and couldn't speak. He knelt down to examine the bodies. When he was finished, he got to his feet again and lit a cigarette with a quivering hand.

'They must have suffered a great deal before they died,' he said with a slight tremor in his voice. 'There are strange cuts on their abdomens. And he finished each of them off with a stab wound to the heart. Around forty-eight hours ago, I'd say. Presumably in the middle of the night, judging by their attire.'

'But their car and luggage have gone!' I cried. 'Who—?'

'The murderer, of course,' cut in Drew. 'After killing them, he made it look as though they went on the run.'

'My God,' moaned Victor. 'To think this happened right above my head, while I was sleeping…'

Drew looked him in the eyes. 'The murderer took a big risk. He must have had a good reason. And yet, it's very strange that he took the time to make his victims suffer before killing them. Particularly since Mr Darnley might have woken up at any moment. Curious. Curious, indeed.'

'What's going on...? Oh! John, my darling. This is awful. Let's get out of here. I don't want to spend another second in this dreadful house...'

John, who still had his arms around his wife, reassured her gently. 'It's over now, darling. We're going home.' He turned to Drew. 'Do you mind?'

Drew shook his head.

'Come, now. The sooner we're out of here, the better.'

John and Elizabeth left the room.

Seeing that his daughter-in-law was somewhat unsteady on her feet, Victor Darnley spoke to Drew. 'I'd better go with them. It's so easy to miss one's footing out there in the snow.'

'All right, but be careful.'

When he was gone, silence descended again.

Drew was shaking his head in desperation.

'I don't understand it at all...'

'Inspector,' said Henry, 'don't let yourself be blinded by what happened to the Latimers. Their deaths aren't necessarily connected to the others.' He stood over the sofa, peering down at the bodies. 'I believe your theory was correct after all.' He pointed at the Latimers. '*They* are the killers we've been searching for. Killers, and frauds.'

Drew's eyes regained their familiar gleam. 'Of course — they must have had their share of enemies, what with their occult nonsense. It makes perfect sense that their deaths aren't connected to the other murders. Why didn't I think of it sooner?'

'Now that the Latimers are dead,' Henry went on, 'there's no reason for me to keep quiet any longer. Let's sit down, shall we? What I have to say to you may take a little while.'

We seated ourselves around the pedestal table. At Henry's request, the ceiling and wall lights were extinguished, so that the only illumination came from the fire in the hearth. Henry felt around under the table, and suddenly the crystal ball lit up.

It was as though everything around it ceased to exist, as though that crystal ball was the centre of its own strange universe.

Drew studied it in fascination. I, too, was positively hypnotised; I had almost forgotten the two corpses lying just across the room.

Henry let us drink in this atmosphere for a moment, then declared, 'Throw in some clever sleight-of-hand and soon enough you'll be ready to believe just about anything. It's nothing to be ashamed of. Plenty of people – noted intellectuals, no less – have been similarly mystified, my father among them. Not only was he mystified, but he also wasted considerable sums of money on those two frauds lying inside the sofa.

'The whole story began with Mrs Darnley's suicide. And it *was* a suicide, not a murder, as was later suggested. Victor lost his mind, his business went bankrupt shortly afterwards, forcing him to rent out part of the house.

'Then came the first mystery: the tenants are disturbed by eerie footsteps in the attic at night, as well as lights appearing in the window of the room where the suicide took place. The solution is very simple: it is, of course, Victor, who is so greatly disturbed that he is keeping vigil in the hope of catching sight of his wife.

'Several tenants later, the house has acquired a sinister reputation. The rumours of the "haunted house" spread far and wide, eventually reaching the ears of the Latimers. As we know, Alice and Patrick Latimer are a pair of fraudulent mediums – with a haunted house, all theirs for the taking! It's like a dream come true; a perfect setting for their séances.

'So they move in. Their neighbour, my father, is a famous writer, who is also recently widowed. The Latimers immediately see the potential, and they begin their performance with a rather brilliant sleight-of-hand trick: Alice is "possessed" by my mother's spirit.'

'So it was a trick?' I said.

'Obviously. First, it's important to note that it's remarkably easy to extract a sheet of paper from a sealed envelope. You just need to slip a long, thin pair of tweezers through the narrow space between flap and envelope, above the seal. You grip one end of the paper, and then twist the tweezers round and round until the paper is completely rolled up. Then you withdraw the tweezers, and the paper will come with them. To replace it, just reverse the process. With a little practice, it can be done very quickly – and even in the dark. Are you beginning to understand now, James?'

'Yes, but—'

'Before Alice goes into her "trance", Patrick tampers briefly with the lamp by the drawing-room window. He slips a bit of metal between the socket and bulb, meaning that whenever the switch is flipped, it blows out all the fuses.

'Alice begins her act, Patrick informs us of his wife's "gifts" and offers my father a demonstration. Father demurs – he is still sceptical at this point – but eventually accepts. He writes a question intended for his late wife onto a piece of paper, slips it into an envelope, which is then sealed and placed on the table. Patrick is close to the window, right beside the gimmicked lamp, so he waits for a convenient bolt of lightning and then flips the switch, causing the short-circuit. During the blackout, he extracts the paper and replaces the envelope on the table before returning to his position by the window. Then the power comes back on.

'I don't know if you remember, James, but at that moment, Patrick seemed to be looking at his shoes. In fact he was looking at the sheet of paper, which he had placed on the floor directly behind the armchair, so nobody else would spot it.

'Seconds later there is another flash of lightning and Patrick flips the switch again – not all the way this time, though, so the fuses don't blow out when the lights come back on.'

'Hold on, Henry. I think I may be able to pick up the thread from there. Patrick uses *this* blackout to replace the sheet of paper in the envelope. Then the lights come back. And then... wait a moment... Ah, yes! When Alice returns to her senses, Patrick whispers something in her ear — obviously the contents of the note. Next, they knock the lamp over, sending it crashing to the floor. It's now unusable, so their blackout trick will never be discovered. And then they wait till the very last moment — until just before they leave, for maximum effect — and Alice discloses your mother's reply. I must admit, it was a clever trick.'

'So clever, in fact, that my father was utterly convinced. Not to mention Victor, who has fostered a belief in the supernatural ever since his wife died.

'A great success for the Latimers. And from then on, Father consults Alice frequently... right here in this room. I won't dwell on all the tricks they pulled on him, but he often told me they had succeeded in contacting Mother.'

Drew smiled. 'I imagine Mrs Latimer was well paid.'

'She was. Embarrassingly so; far beyond whatever you might imagine.'

'But, Henry, if you knew all along that they were charlatans, why didn't you say anything?'

'Don't you remember the rows we used to have? I tried to tell him of my suspicions, but he wouldn't listen. And so we argued.'

'Your suspicions?' I said incredulously. 'Why didn't you explain how the tricks were done?'

Henry blushed. 'I couldn't, James. I just couldn't. From the moment they arrived, the Latimers had me over a barrel.'

'How come?'

'I was madly in love with Alice. We... were lovers. I couldn't resist her, James. It was simply impossible. She bewitched me, I suppose. She told me she was dazzled by my magic tricks.

But, in fact, she knew immediately that I was the only one who might know what she and her husband were up to. She was very ambitious, and so was I; she took full advantage of that. I can hear her now: "Together we'll conquer the world, my darling. But first, I need to make a name for myself. Henry, my love, you have to help me! And whatever you do, you mustn't let on to your father that we're taking him for a ride! He's a well-connected man, he'll spread the word to all sorts of people. What do you mean, *fraud*? Can't you see how happy he is to be in contact with his departed wife again? The money? But, my dearest darling, we shall need every penny of it to launch our double act! Yes, my sweet, I'll ask for a divorce very soon. You know full well that Patrick means nothing to me; he hasn't ever since I met you… Soon, darling, soon. I promise."

'I didn't know what to do. I was caught between a rock and a hard place. On the one hand, my father was paying out ridiculous sums of money to the Latimers. I pitied him for his credulity, but I couldn't tell him the whole story… I tried to reason with him, but that just made him angry. And on the other hand, Alice. Alice, with her passion and her promises.

'To attract clients, she came up with the idea of reprising the "ghost in the attic" business. Naturally, she had known all along that Victor was the one going up there. But can you guess who took his place? Why, I did, of course. I protested, naturally… but I could never say no to Alice. Let's just say she had ways of convincing me.'

'So it was *you*,' I exclaimed. '*You* were the one that John, Victor and your father heard walking about in the attic!'

'I was,' said Henry, his face in his hands.

'But there was nobody up there. John was quite convinced of that.'

'At the last moment I climbed out of the window and up onto the gable. It was child's play.'

'But the window was locked on the inside when he searched the room.'

'I pulled it shut behind me, and Alice managed to lock it discreetly while pretending to search the room.'

'Clever,' I said, annoyed that I had not thought of it.

'We repeated the performance several times for different audiences. The Latimers did very well out of it, as you can imagine. For Victor, this midnight visitor was quite obviously his wife – the wife he had been waiting for all these years!

'Eventually, I could no longer bring myself to take advantage of Victor and all these other people – especially my father. I was at my wits' end.'

'I remember it well. You were very difficult to talk to at the time.'

'The rows between me and my father got worse, and Alice was still refusing to get a divorce.

'One day, I made up my mind: either Alice left with me right away, or I would tell everyone what they had been up to. I went to see her and issued an ultimatum. She was crying, begging, going through her entire repertoire to try and convince me, but I stood my ground. That's when I was knocked unconscious.

'I came to, gagged and tied to the bed. Patrick was sitting beside me with a long, dull knife in his hand.

'I was petrified. Not only by the sight of the knife, but by the way Patrick and Alice were looking at each other. In the blink of an eye, I saw it all. Alice had seduced me in order to control me – and Patrick had known all along. I was just a plaything to those monsters. There was nothing they were not capable of.

'I was nothing to her. She only had eyes for Patrick. I can still picture the way she smiled at him when she said, "I'll leave you to it, darling." That's when Patrick tried to buy my silence. I refused. He didn't force me. There was a murderous look in his eyes; I knew he had been planning to kill me from the start. "Well then," he said, "you leave me no choice."

'But his cruelty caused him to make a mistake. Instead of killing me with a single blow, he slowly plunged the knife into my belly.

'By that time, I was quite familiar with the fakirs who have developed techniques for piercing their abdomens with a sword. They keep the blade dull, and pierce the flesh slowly, so the vital organs are pushed out of the way and only the muscle and tissue is perforated.

'I realised this knowledge might save my life. I bit down on my gag – the pain was excruciating – and eventually passed out.

'When at last I came to, the pain in my stomach was almost unbearable. I could hear a strange, monotonous sound – Patrick was digging a hole. He thought I was dead, and was preparing to bury me. There were trees all around – we were in the woods. Then he dragged me by the arm and dropped me into the shallow grave; it was scarcely more than three feet deep. As I fell, I filled my lungs and arched my back to give myself a small reserve of air. If I had tried to get out, Patrick would have finished me off with the shovel, so I decided it was better to play dead and try to dig myself out when he was gone.

'As he shovelled the dirt on top of me, I thought of Houdini. Houdini had been buried six feet under and lived to tell the tale! Of course I didn't have all his tools at my disposal – quite the contrary – but I was buried only half as deep! I had as good a chance as anybody. I began to flex my muscles, all the while controlling my breathing – there was only the tiniest amount of air between my arched back and the bottom of the grave.'

'And you made it out of there,' said Drew, clearly fascinated by my friend's tale.

'Barely,' said Henry. 'The hardest part was overcoming my fear. Not an easy thing to do when you're buried alive, I can tell you.'

'This explains everything,' said Drew. 'Your father saw Patrick carrying you into the woods to bury you. He followed, and Patrick knocked him out with the shovel. The Latimers must have been terrified when they found out Mr White had survived the attack; when he came to his senses, we would make the obvious connection between Henry's disappearance and the corpse seen in the woods.

'What were they to do? They couldn't let anybody know that Henry was dead. There'd be an investigation, a search of the woods, which would, of course, be very dangerous. They needed to come up with a solution quickly – before Mr White regained consciousness. And they did: they would say they had caught sight of Henry, looking troubled as he waited for a train at Paddington. This was a brilliant idea; not only would it convince everyone that Henry was still alive, but it would also make us think *Henry* was responsible for the attack on his father, and had run away.

'This was the most risk-free option; after all, as far as they were concerned, Henry was dead, so there was nobody to dispute their version of events. It was a fine plan, and might even have worked – except for one thing.'

Henry smiled. 'The truly incredible coincidence that caused James to bump into me at Oxford Station. At that time, I had no idea my father had been attacked. I was so sick of everything; the woman I loved had made a fool of me and left me for dead. My relationship with my father was intolerable. What's more, I had assisted the Latimers with their criminal scheme... I wandered for a while, before making the decision to leave the country. That's why I found myself at Oxford Station that day.'

'You spoke to me on the platform, Henry,' I said. 'Do you remember? You said, "People are just too cruel. I'm leaving."'

Henry nodded.

'The irony!' cried Drew. 'The Latimers claimed they saw you

in London at half-past twelve, while at that exact moment you really *were* seen by your friend at Oxford!'

'I wonder what they thought when they heard that,' I said. 'Did they think I'd experienced some kind of vision? Or that Henry had come back from the dead?'

'Maybe,' Drew suggested, 'they went to check the grave in the woods and found that your body was missing. Of course, we've no way of knowing.' He paused. 'Three years pass, during which the Latimers continue their criminal career. Now, I'd like to know how they managed to kill Bob Farr in that sealed room. And what was Bob Farr doing in England anyway?'

'When I was in America,' Henry said, 'I spent most of my time dreaming of coming back to England. But I couldn't return without plotting a little revenge on my dear friends, the Latimers. I decided to take advantage of my likeness to Bob in order to spring a surprise on them. The idea was for him to pay them a visit, and then for me to make an appearance. Can you imagine the effect? The Latimers had worked so hard to convince other people of the existence of spirits, and now they were going to encounter the spirit of the man they had murdered – not once, but twice!

'Naturally I warned Bob that these were dangerous people, and wouldn't be afraid to make him disappear. "Don't worry," he said to me. "If they try anything, I'll be sure to teach them a lesson." He left for England, promising to telephone me every couple of days.

'I don't know what happened after that, but I can take an educated guess. I assume they captured him, and held him prisoner. I can imagine their conversation:

'"It's not a ghost, Alice. He wasn't quite dead when I buried him, that's all."

'"That's all? What do you mean, that's all?"

'"We'll have to get rid of him, of course. But I have an idea.

Instead of making him disappear, let's make him *re*appear..."

"'Are you mad? You'll get us hanged!'"

"'No, listen to me, my dear: we are going to suggest to Victor and Arthur that Mrs Darnley was murdered, and that her ghost – which has been haunting the attic ever since she died, let's not forget – is out for revenge. We'll suggest an experiment in the haunted room, where we seal up the door. Then, when Henry's corpse appears can you imagine the effect it will have? Think of the publicity!'"

"'Yes, but isn't it terribly dangerous? Won't they suspect us?'"

"'Not for a moment. Here's my plan—'"

Henry paused his story. 'It must have happened this way, or close enough.'

'All right,' said Drew with a nod, 'it all fits together so far. But what then? How did they replace the seal after murdering Bob in the haunted room?'

Henry turned to me. 'James, do you remember that strange sensation you experienced when you went up to the attic the second time? The corridor was out of proportion.'

The clouds in my memory finally lifted. 'Yes,' I cried, 'that was it! But I don't see…'

'You must remember that I wasn't there at the time,' Henry continued, 'but the information I heard about it after the fact was enough for me to piece together what happened. This crime was a *tour de force*, so to speak, which only a pair of professional illusionists could have performed. So, how did they do it?

'The layout of the house was very helpful. A corridor leading up to a curtain, behind which is a blank wall. Four doors along the right-hand side of the corridor, each leading to an identical room – apart from the first, which is cluttered with furniture. Also, note that the doors are the same colour as the walls, which are panelled with dark oak. The four white doorknobs stand out clearly.

'What did you see the first time you went up to that corridor? Light spilling out of the last door – which hung open – and made the other three doorknobs gleam. That is all you saw.

'The open door was in fact the *third*. The Latimers had brought the curtain forward, shortening the corridor and concealing the fourth door. They had also removed three doorknobs and fixed them at regular intervals along the remaining stretch of corridor.

'Thanks to their use of lighting, it was a perfect optical illusion. You were under the impression that you were in a corridor lined with four doors along the right-hand wall, the last of which was open. And, to conceal the trick with the doorknobs, remember that Alice positioned herself along that side of the corridor, guiding you quickly into the third room – which you took for the fourth room, the haunted room.

'Shortly before nine o'clock, Patrick must have murdered Bob, who was tied up in the *real* haunted room. By that time, the doorknobs and curtain were already in place. At half-past nine, Alice leaves for ten minutes with the candelabra, the sealing wax, and the infamous coin. Incidentally, this is the only time Father lets the coin out of his possession. You can guess how she spent those ten minutes: she was sealing the fourth room, where Bob's murdered body lay, and placing the candelabra in the third room so its light would create the illusion I've already described.

'She returns downstairs. Patrick goes to fetch his coat and Alice leads the others up to the attic, to what they believe is the haunted room. Patrick arrives last, and he is acting strangely, with his coat and hat concealing his features. This is an important part of the plan, to create the idea that he might actually have been an impostor.

'Everybody leaves – with the exception of Patrick, of course – and the door is sealed up. Naturally, Alice is the one to do this; the seals must be identical to those she has already placed on the fourth door.

'A short while later, while everyone is waiting on the floor below, Patrick leaves the room. He carefully removes all trace of the seals as he goes, then replaces the curtain and the doorknobs in their original positions. It now appears that Bob Farr has appeared by magic in the fourth room — when in fact he has been in there all along. Note also that the dead man was dressed up in a hat and coat identical to Patrick's.

'Patrick then goes downstairs to the hall to prepare for his next role — that of a man who's been knocked unconscious by an unknown assailant when he went to fetch his coat.

'Yes, this crime is a masterpiece all right. The only time there is any possible risk of anybody spotting what they were up to was during that first climb up to the attic. But I'm sure they would have planned something in case anybody noticed the curious arrangement of the curtain and doorknobs. And remember, nobody had even the slightest suspicion there might be a corpse in one of the rooms! You were all too distracted by the sinister atmosphere the Latimers had created. Even Victor, who knew the house well, was too overwhelmed by the idea of reuniting with his late wife to notice that the corridor was slightly shorter than it used to be. And by the time Patrick has replaced the curtain and the doorknobs, there won't be any evidence of the Latimers' deception; Bob's body will be found behind that sealed fourth door, and the whole thing will seem to be the work of evil spirits.

'In fact, it will become apparent that no mortal could have entered that sealed room at all. And I must confess, James, that if you hadn't mentioned the strange feeling you got when you went up to the corridor the second time, I never would have worked out how they did it — even though I knew full well the Latimers were responsible.'

'Indeed,' Drew conceded, 'this is a truly remarkable crime. But if we'd spent a little longer investigating that corridor I'm sure we would have found traces left from moving the doorknobs and the curtain rail.'

'I would be very surprised,' said Henry. 'Patrick was careful to remove all traces. Don't forget, Inspector, that you're dealing with a couple of professional illusionists. Imagine how careful they must have been, knowing that their lives were on the line. Of course, you could always take another look, but I think the most you will find is a nail that was used to temporarily secure one of the doorknobs in place.'

'There isn't much point now, is there?' said Drew, nodding towards the sofa. 'The Latimers aren't going to stand trial.'

'I don't know who killed them,' said Henry with a smile, 'but let's just say I'm in no hurry to see their killer brought to justice.' He was silent for a moment. 'Poor Bob. I never should have let him go. Before he came to England, he promised to telephone regularly. And he did, to begin with. But then I stopped hearing from him. I realised immediately that the Latimers must have got to him somehow. So I took the next plane, and… the rest you know.'

'But Henry, why didn't you accuse them publicly? Your father might still be alive if you had.'

'Yes,' answered Henry, 'that's true. But I had no idea what else they were capable of. And there was no evidence, you understand. My return must have really put the wind up them, since they thought they'd killed me twice already. I wanted to let them stew, then maybe they'd do something stupid and give themselves away. Alice had a nervous breakdown, after all.

'Now that I've given it some thought, I believe they got the wrong man when they killed my father. Obviously I was their real target. They had plenty of motive, after all. Damn it, if only I'd known what they were up to…'

Drew did not take his eyes off the crystal ball as he lit another cigarette. His face had assumed an expression of absolute serenity.

As far as he was concerned, Henry had explained everything.

'I must admit,' he eventually said, 'that those two murderers demonstrated incredible virtuosity. Criminals of their calibre are exceedingly rare. But that leaves us with your father's murder. I should very much like to know how they got into and out of the house without leaving a single footprint in the snow. Can you explain it?'

'No, I can't,' said Henry. 'At least, not yet. I just need to work it out…'

Suddenly, Drew's face fell. His mouth opened, but no sound came out; he was frozen to the spot.

'What is it, Inspector?' Henry asked softly.

'I… They… The Latimers have been dead for two days. They couldn't have killed your father. He was murdered barely twenty-four hours ago. They couldn't have done it. It's impossible.'

2
THE PSYCHOLOGIST LOSES HIS MIND

A HEAVY SILENCE HUNG IN THAT ROOM. Drew was distraught, puffing heavily on his cigarette till a cloud formed above his head. Henry was wringing his hands; sweat rolled down his forehead and a vein throbbed in his temple.

'Who was it, then?' I snapped. 'Who?'

Henry gave the merest hint of a smile. 'There's only one person in the world who might have done it. Just one.'

I don't know why, but the look on his face sent a chill down my spine. His face had turned a strange colour and there was a frightening, glassy glow in his eyes.

'The man who astonished the whole world,' he continued. 'The man who is immortal.'

'Who?' demanded Inspector Drew.

Henry's face now bore a look of triumph. When he spoke, his voice was unrecognisable. 'Harry Houdini.'

Drew stared at Henry for a long time. 'Harry Houdini,' he repeated. 'But…'

A silence fell once more. Henry nervously lit a cigarette, swallowed a few times, then began, 'On his deathbed, Houdini promised his wife that he would send her a message from beyond the grave. She waited for it endlessly – and in vain. It seemed that the only confinement Houdini had failed to escape was the realm of the dead. Big mistake! Houdini kept his final promise. The only reason he did not make himself known was that he did not know who he was! Three years after his death, Houdini was reincarnated. That was 1929, the year I was born…

'This is rather difficult to explain, because it wasn't a random reincarnation, but a familial one. You see, Houdini came back as one of his own descendants.' Henry looked admiringly at Inspector Drew. 'If not for you, Inspector, and your brilliant abilities as a psychologist – your almost supernatural insight – nobody would ever have known. Not even Houdini himself.

'You see, I am Houdini.'

My heart stopped. Drew and I were paralysed with terror. My friend had truly gone insane; he really believed he was Harry Houdini.

'I owe everything to you, Inspector,' Henry continued, shaking Drew by the hand. 'Again, if not for you I never would have known who I really was. Your speech the other day, your in-depth investigation, demonstrated it admirably. I am Houdini! Houdini, King of Escape Artists! How else to explain the remarkable resemblance? And the name "White", derived from Father's real name – Weiss? A Weiss who happened to be born in Budapest, too!' He looked down at his own wrists with an expression of awe. 'Houdini's blood flows through these veins. I am Houdini. The Great Houdini!

'Yes, Inspector, I owe it all to you! If not for you, I wouldn't have known. Wouldn't have known that the one who killed my mother had to die, and die by my very hands. You see, my mother was everything to me. Her death was a dreadful ordeal, I cannot begin to tell you…

'And when I realised thanks to you that I was really Houdini, I understood that my father had forfeited his right to live. Thanks to him, the woman who gave birth to Houdini was dead – killed in a car crash three years ago! Houdini had no choice but to seek vengeance, even against his own father. He had to kill the man responsible for this dreadful crime.'

Faced with the true horror of the situation, Drew buried his face in his hands. The so-called 'Psychologist' was now responsible for this descent into mania. Not only had he driven Henry mad, he had supplied him with a motive for murder. It was scarcely imaginable; a police inspector creating a murderer. He couldn't speak. He was devastated.

'Henry,' I stammered, 'this can't be true. You spent the whole evening with me, don't you remember? You couldn't have…'

'Yes, James, it was I who killed him. It was I who *had* to kill him. And I must confess that my murder was a masterpiece… a masterpiece of simplicity and ingenuity.

'Since Bob's death, Father – along with plenty of other villagers – went to bed with a loaded gun by his side. Remember, James, we were just singing "Happy Birthday" when the telephone rang; I went out to answer. I told you it was a wrong number, but it wasn't. It was my father. And do you know what he said?

'"Henry! Send help, quickly! I was cleaning my rifle and… it went off… get an ambulance right away… if you don't, I'll die… but there might still be a chance… Quick, Henry!"

'You must remember, I had been planning to murder my father for several days, and here was a unique opportunity. By refusing to sound the alarm, I was going to avenge my mother's death at last.

'And then, James, we played a game of chess. Naturally my mind was elsewhere, otherwise – as I'm sure you'll admit – you never would have won. While we played, I went through the situation in my mind. There was very little chance he would be able to reach anybody else by telephone. And why should he want to? After all, I had already told him I would take care of it.

'It was an accident. However, thanks to me, it became a murder – don't forget that. And we had to discover the body before it began to snow again, so there would be no footprints – another magical, supernatural murder! A crime worthy of Houdini. But you see, I needed it to *seem* like a murder.

'When I was with the circus, I knew a ventriloquist. He tried to teach me the art, but I was never very good at it. However, I *did* realise I was rather skilled at imitating voices.

'Shortly before eleven o'clock, after finishing our game of chess, I telephoned Father. He didn't answer; by then he was dead. And so I telephoned Victor, impersonating Father: "The killer... oh, my head... there was a noise... I woke up... there was a shadow... a gunshot... It hurts, Victor, come quickly. I'm dying. Quickly..."

'You know the rest. I must admit, though, I was a little nervous when it turned out Father was still alive. Fortunately, he was past saving. The delay had proved fatal after all.

'Of course, *I* was the one who opened the door leading to the back garden. Ha! The killer fled without leaving a trace in the snow! A crime worthy of Houdini.

'One last detail, James: do you know why we didn't hear the gunshot? Because we were singing our drunken songs at the top of our lungs!

'I'm telling you all this, my friends, because I know I can count on your discretion. Inspector, I'll never be able to thank you enough for introducing me to my true nature. Thank you. A thousand times, thank you!'

I was curled up in my chair, hoping the ground would swallow me so I might no longer hear Henry's terrible voice.

'The Latimers had killed my friend, Bob. At first I didn't know whether to hand them in to the police or to bring about my own retribution. I thought about this for quite some time. I'd seen them loading their belongings into the car, they would be leaving soon; I had to act quickly... So I slipped into their room. I knocked them unconscious while they were sleeping. I tied them up, gagged them... they were dreadfully frightened when they woke to find me standing over them, knife in hand. You should have seen their faces! It was a most exquisite revenge, watching them squirm as they waited for me to inflict the same fate they had reserved for me three years ago.

'I finished them both off with the knife, but not before adding a few little buttonholes here and there, just so they knew what it felt like. Yes, they got the end they deserved, that wretched pair who brought so much misery to our little village.

'I couldn't carry them downstairs; Victor would have heard me. So I installed them in the sofa on a temporary basis, until an opportunity to make them disappear presented itself. Still, it took me a while to pull out all those springs — I was pressed for time, and needed to get rid of them… so I threw them out of the window, threw them as far as I could.

'Their car and its contents are currently at the bottom of the river, not too far from here. I… What is it, James? James, are you crying? And you, Inspector — what's the matter with you? Pull yourselves together! You are in the presence of Houdini! Harry Houdini, King of Escape Artists! The man who cheated death! The man who—'

I could stand it no longer; I keeled over in a faint. I just had time to see Drew drawing his revolver.

3

LAST RESPECTS

'All right, Inspector Drew, so somebody stole your car. Why mobilise the entire county's police just to find your car? It's one in the morning! You've got two fresh corpses on your hands, and all you're bothered about is car theft…'

'Shut up.'

'Very well. We're finished here anyway, the bodies can be removed. To think we've been searching for these two beauties up and down the country and here they were, under our noses this whole time.'

'One more word out of you, Sergeant, and I—'

'All right, boss. Understood. I think that Stevens fellow is coming to his senses, anyway. But you haven't told me yet how he came to pass out in the first place. Or how you got that black eye, for that matter.'

'Sergeant, that's enough! Clear the room, I want everybody out. And don't come back under any circumstances – unless you've got some news about my car.'

I started to collect myself. The police withdrew from the drawing room and the inspector came and stood over me. His face bore a quite remarkable bruise.

'Are you feeling any better?'

'I am. But what happened to Henry?'

'Wait until we're alone,' he said, glancing nervously at the retreating police officers. 'There, now we can talk. You see, you and I are the only ones who know that Henry's the killer. Just as I was about to arrest him, he threw the crystal ball in my face. By the time I came to, he was gone – and my car was gone with him.'

With that, a police officer burst back into the room. 'Chief, we've found your car. Somebody spotted it en route to London.

'Quick,' Drew breathed, 'let's go. That means you too, I'll probably need your assistance.'

It was three in the morning before we caught up with him.

'There he is, Inspector. On the bridge. We can't get any nearer, he's armed. He's already injured two of our men. What shall we do?'

'Nothing. Tell the men to stay where they are. You're sure he can't get away?'

'Quite sure,' said the constable, looking surprised. 'We've got officers stationed at both ends of the bridge. He can't escape. Unless he jumps into the Thames, but that would be suicide. As for your car, sir, I'm afraid—'

'Forget about my car,' yelled Drew. 'Just do what I tell you. Right, I'm going to approach. Don't let anybody move.'

'Inspector, that's suicide! He'll shoot you down! He's got a gun, he's already—'

Drew looked as though he was about to punch his subordinate on the nose, but relented at the last moment. Then he headed for the bridge.

'Wait, Inspector! I'm coming with you!'

Drew turned back to me. 'He's got the pistol from my glove box, you know. It's a fearsome weapon. He's very dangerous.'

'I know that. But I'm his best friend. He won't hurt me.'

Drew hesitated a moment, then beckoned me to follow. The officers near the bridge looked at us both as though we were walking into certain death. Drew reached the bridge, and I quickened my pace to catch up to him.

A few hours earlier, Henry and I were having dinner together. Henry, my lifelong friend. Henry, who had become a monster. Henry, who was about to spring at us from behind one of these pillars at any moment…

The Thames flowed peacefully below us, sparkling in the silvery moonlight.

Henry, a killer! My God!

'There he is,' said Drew. 'That shadow behind the pillar there. Keep walking normally, young man. Act as though nothing has happened.'

'Stay here, Inspector. Let me go alone.'

'Out of the question.'

'All right, but walk behind me at least.'

I could now make out Henry's face among the shadows, but my friend was no longer recognisable. His face was a mask of madness and terror.

'Don't come any closer, James!' he called out, brandishing the revolver.

'It's me, Henry! I'm your friend!'

'Stop!'

'Henry, you're ill. You need help. Come on now. Give me the gun.'

I was a few feet away from him; I could see his index finger tightening around the trigger. I looked him straight in the eyes.

He hung his head. The weapon fell from his hand.

'James,' he said in a pitiful whisper.

Then he climbed over the parapet and dived into the darkness. A distant splash was the only sound.

Drew went over to lean against the parapet and I joined him. The smooth, black surface of the Thames looked peaceful and undisturbed once more.

'It's over,' said Drew. 'There's nothing we can do for him now. Maybe it's better this way.'

'You know, Inspector, Henry was a good man. Nobody can be allowed to know that he killed his father, do you hear me? Nobody. And the Latimers got what they deserved.'

Drew placed a hand on my shoulder.

'Henry wasn't the one who killed his father. It was a foolish police inspector who called himself "The Psychologist"... who thought he was so clever... Young man, you've no idea how disgusted I am with myself. If not for my wife and children, I think I might follow your friend over the parapet. Your friend, whom *I* drove to murder...

'You have nothing to worry about. Nobody will ever know what really happened. I'll see to it that Mr White's death is recorded as an accident, after which your friend committed suicide. As for the Latimers, their deaths will be easy enough to explain: one of the people they were duping simply turned on them and took revenge.'

On the banks of the Thames, searchlights pierced the darkness; they swept across the surface of the water like luminous brushstrokes.

Footsteps echoed all around; the other officers were approaching.

'Come on,' said Drew. 'They'll never find your friend alive. Come with me, I'll take you home.'

'No, thank you, Inspector. I don't want to go home just yet. I need to be alone.'

Two days later, Mr and Mrs Stevens reported the disappearance of their son, James. He was never found.

PART FIVE

EPILOGUE

Amazing. Somehow, Dr Twist found his way out of the maze. I could hardly believe it; his solution seemed to be the only natural and logical one. And yet, the whole thing fitted together so perfectly, it was as though the original author had known the answers all along – which was certainly not the case, I can assure you. Not only had he provided explanations for the deaths of Bob Farr and Arthur White, but he also managed to shed some light on all of Henry's strange behaviour.

There were two possibilities: either Dr Twist really was extraordinary, or else I'd somehow had the solution tucked away in my subconscious all along. Typically, my daily output was three pages or so. I took many breaks in order to gather my thoughts, and consulted all kinds of reference books. This time, though, I had written non-stop every evening for two weeks, using only one resource: the Houdini biography.

I could hardly believe it myself. And why had Dr Twist made James Stevens go missing at the very end? It added nothing to the story, and was actually rather ridiculous.

Come to think of it, the covering letter was strange too. *There could be only one explanation, after all. I admit that I had the benefit of some outside assistance, not in solving the mystery but in writing the epilogue. I shall say no more for the moment. We can discuss everything at our next meeting.* What was that all about?

Better not to waste time trying to fathom it out. I decided to call him instead.

Just as I was dialling his number, I had a change of heart. Better to let him stew for two or three days – if I were to call him as soon as I had finished reading, it would only flatter his ego, and I wasn't in the mood to hear him crowing on the other end of the phone. I was frankly a little irritated that he had solved the mystery so quickly after I – 'John Carter', mystery author extraordinaire – bet that he couldn't.

It was almost noon and Jimmy still wasn't back. We had planned to lunch at the White Horse, but I didn't have much appetite. Presumably Jimmy didn't either, given his absence.

I hadn't set foot outside yet that day; it occurred to me that a walk in the fresh air might do me some good. My house is located deep in the countryside, over a mile from the nearest village. It's a perfect setting for peace and solitude; I find it particularly inspiring.

I strolled over gently rolling fields, deep in thought. A few confused ideas cluttered my brain, but eventually these began to subside. Soon my mood was calm and serene. I was in such a good mood that I completely lost track of time; it was well after two in the afternoon when I got home.

As I entered the study, I found Jimmy sitting at my desk. He jumped to his feet when he saw me; in his hands were the papers I had received from Dr Twist.

'Have you read it?' I said.

'Read?' He glanced at the papers in his hand, then replaced them on the desk. 'No, I was just waiting for you. I picked these up automatically. I haven't read them.'

'Well, I'm sorry to have kept you. I was walking around and completely missed lunch.'

'It doesn't matter, I'm not hungry anyway. But I'd better go now; I have an appointment.'

*

Jimmy did not come back that day. Nor did he come the next day, or the day after that. I was starting to worry about his curious absence, so I telephoned his apartment. No answer. Then I called the concierge at his building.

'Could I speak to Jimmy Lessing, please?'

'Mr Lessing no longer lives here,' she answered in a surly voice.

'What do you mean, no longer lives there?'

'He's gone. He left two days ago.'

'Well, where on earth has he gone?'

'I don't know, he didn't leave an address. All I know is that he's left the country. He mentioned something about America, but I can't tell you anything more than that.'

I hung up. I could feel the blood rushing to my face. Jimmy had left the country, completely without warning! What did it mean?

The ringing telephone brought me back to my senses.

'Yes?' I growled.

'Ronald?'

'Dr Twist! I'm so glad to hear from you. I got the papers you sent, and I have to congratulate you. I never would have thought—'

Alan Twist cut me off. 'Can you come and see me later on this afternoon?'

'Let me just check... Yes, I think I'm free. I can stop by at around five o'clock if that suits.'

'Yes, that's fine. I – Ah! Doctor! I'd better hang up, Ronald. My doctor has just arrived. I'll see you later.'

'No tobacco. None at all!' Dr Twist fumed. 'He says it's bad for my heart. I ask you! As if a little puff here and there could do me any harm. Besides, it helps me think! And do you know what else he told me, old Doctor Death? That I should consider myself lucky I'm still allowed to have whisky – in moderation, of course. To hell with that.'

With these words, he produced his large meerschaum pipe, stuffed it with tobacco and lit it. Then he sat back in his armchair and contemplated the sea, which could be made out in the distance beyond his French window. The window frames rattled in the wind; the distant waves raged and crashed.

'What weather,' he continued, drawing his smoking jacket tight around his shoulders. 'A drop of whisky will help to stave off the chill. I'll do the honours.'

He stood up, uncurling his wiry frame from the chair, and went to the drinks cabinet to pour the whisky. It must be something more than gardening that keeps him in such excellent shape, I thought.

The whisky did indeed hit the spot, but I wasn't about to let it distract me.

'Dr Twist,' I said, 'why did you have James Stevens disappear at the end of the story? I could see no reason for it.'

Twist stared at me for a long time from behind his *pince-nez*. 'I don't know if you recall our last conversation,' he said, running a hand through his silver hair, 'but I suggested that you write a mystery story without a solution.'

'That's exactly what I did.'

He shook his head. 'No, no, you didn't. You didn't play by the rules. You wrote a story knowing precisely how it would end.'

'I assure you, I didn't,' I protested.

'Wrong. There were so many clues leading to that conclusion. There could have been no other possible explanation. It was so obvious that I spotted it almost immediately.'

'Dr Twist, I can assure you that—'

'You're also going to tell me,' he interrupted, 'that you invented Arthur White. Arthur White, the famous novelist!'

A light flashed in my memory. 'Wait a moment – Arthur White. Yes, now that you mention it, the name *does* ring a bell...'

'I thought it might,' he said, pluming a ribbon of smoke from his pipe. 'Arthur White did indeed exist. He died accidentally, while cleaning a rifle. That was in 1951. Two days later, his son Henry – who was deeply affected by his father's death – committed suicide by hurling himself into the Thames... just like in your story.'

'I wasn't living in England at the time,' I informed him. 'But, yes, now that you mention it, the details are coming back to me. So you're saying I must have unconsciously used the facts of that case when I was writing the story? Incredible.'

Dr Twist cleared his throat. 'You didn't write a story at all. You narrated the events as they really happened. When I finished reading, I immediately phoned my old friend Hurst, a retired Scotland Yard Chief Inspector. We had a long conversation; he remembered very well the death of the author, White, and the son's suicide. I then gave him another version of events; the version contained in your story. Can you guess what he said to me?

'No? Well, the official version of events had it that Arthur White's death was accidental. Until one day around eight years ago, when Inspector Drew was lying on his deathbed and decided to reveal the truth for the first time.'

'So Drew was real too? How bizarre! I could have sworn I'd made him up...'

'My dear Ronald, you didn't make *any* of it up.' He adjusted his *pince-nez*. 'Not Arthur White, nor his son Henry, nor James Stevens, who disappeared without trace the day after his friend's suicide. Every single character in your story really existed. Of course, some of the names are slightly different, but apart from that the whole drama unfolded exactly as it did in your story.

'Naturally, Drew's confession was never made public. You

can imagine what the press would have made of it: following an accusation from a Scotland Yard inspector, the son of a famous author comes to believe he is a reincarnation of Houdini, then murders his father! What a scandal it would have created.

'Apart from a few nuances here and there, the text I sent to you describes the outcome of that sinister affair just as it happened. I pieced it together using Inspector Drew's statement, which Hurst shared with me. Just as I said in my letter to you, I had solved the mystery, but I had a little help in writing the epilogue. Yes, this little drama unfolded just as you and I wrote it.

'And the day after Henry White's death, in December 1951, James Stevens disappeared. He was never seen again.'

As the echo of these words faded, Dr Twist looked me straight in the eye. He continued, 'This, my dear Ronald, raises a question. How could you possibly have known this story? Because you knew it; there can be no question of coincidence, I'm sure you'll agree.'

I felt uneasy. I tried in vain to reorder my confused thoughts. 'Dr Twist,' I said after a long moment, 'I can assure you I wrote that story purely by instinct. All I used was a book on Houdini...

'Wait a moment. I'm about fifty years old – just as James Stevens would be if he were still alive. You see, I know nothing of my childhood or adolescence. One day in March 1953, Canadian police simply "found" me. I was wandering down a road – a long road – and I couldn't answer any of their questions. I didn't know a thing. Absolutely nothing. Not who I was, or where I came from. I had no identity papers. They tried to find out who I was, of course, but they didn't get anywhere. I didn't match any missing persons reports in either the United States or Canada. They guessed I was about twenty-five years old, and I eventually took the name "Ronald Bowers". But I remain an amnesiac to this day. I've consulted all kinds of specialists over the years – all in vain. Since then, I've learned to accept my condition. I left Canada for England in the early sixties, found work as a journalist, and then — well, you know the rest of my career.

'Do you really think I could be this James Stevens, who disappeared in 1951? The dates are a perfect fit! I can hardly believe it…'

Dr Twist sat slumped in his chair, his eyes closed. A look of dreamy satisfaction crossed his face. He adjusted his *pince-nez* again, then smiled at me. 'It could be, my dear Ronald. It could be. When I realised your story wasn't fiction at all, and that James Stevens had disappeared mysteriously in 1951, I started asking a few questions about your background. That's how I learned that you're an amnesi – well, that you suffer with amnesia, and that your origins are a bit of a mystery. Yes, my friend, I think there's a good chance that you are James Stevens.' He paused, then added, 'Either way, we'll know soon enough.'

I was speechless.

Dr Twist leaned sideways, grabbing a large envelope from a nearby table, which he brandished triumphantly.

'I asked Hurst to send me some extracts from his file on the White case —including a photograph of James Stevens.' He studied the unopened envelope. 'It came this morning, just before I phoned you. I wanted you to open it.'

With my heart pounding, I grabbed the envelope from his hand, ripped it open and took out the papers. After a moment's sifting through them, I gave a cry of triumph. 'It's me! James Stevens! Look at this photograph, Dr Twist. It's me – minus a few years, of course. So I *am* James Stevens.' I took my wallet from my inside pocket, and extracted from it a small photograph. Holding the two side by side, I said, 'Look here. This photograph is me at about thirty years old. Compare it to this one here – there's no doubt about it. I am James Stevens!'

'The faces are identical,' said Dr Twist with a nod.

While he was examining the photographs, I confided, 'To think I'd begun to suspect Jimmy Lessing – do you know him? He used to be a playwright, but he's fallen on hard times. We'd developed a sort of collaborative partnership. He used to give me ideas for my novels. And I wondered if it might have been one of *his* stories that had seeped into my unconscious. He's not English by birth either; he's American. So I wondered if perhaps he was James Stevens – or even Henry White! It was a possibility, after all; three days ago I caught him reading the solution you sent me, and since then he's disappeared. It looks as though he's left the country...'

Dr Twist did not seem to be listening. Looking at me rather vaguely, he observed, 'You wrote the story in a very interesting way, you know. I'm talking about your narrator – James Stevens. He's a difficult character to pin down. Rather a dull sort of person, bereft of passion, taste or humanity... The only aspect of his personality that emerges in the story is his misogyny: all the women he discusses are stupid, silly, authoritarian, insipid or deceitful. There's only one woman he describes favourably – Mrs White. Mrs White, whose kindness and gentleness of spirit clearly made an impact on him...'

Irritated at being ignored, I raised my voice, 'As I was saying, Jimmy Lessing has left the country and I'd begun to suspect he might be the real Henry White. But Henry White drowned in the Thames back in 1951.'

'Or so we thought,' said Twist. 'His body was never found, of course. But the water was freezing... no normal human being could have survived it.'

'Well,' I sighed, 'it doesn't matter now. I can still hardly believe it – I'm James Stevens. Put yourself in my shoes, Dr Twist – Doctor? What's the matter?'

His expression had darkened. There was a look of great sadness in his eyes, and beads of sweat had begun forming on his forehead. He was staring intently at the photograph from the file.

'The man in this photograph is you, Ronald. There can be no doubt about it. But there's an inscription on the back. This isn't a picture of James Stevens at all. It's Henry White.'

About the Author

Photo courtesy of Paul Halter

Paul Halter is a French crime writer, known for his locked room mysteries.

His first published novel, *La Quatrieme Porte* (*The Fourth Door*) was published in 1988 and won the Prix de Cognac, given for detective literature. The following year, his novel *Le Brouillard Rouge* (*Red Mist*) won the Prix du Roman d'Aventures.

Bedford Square Publishers is an independent publisher of fiction and non-fiction, founded in 2022 in the historic streets of Bedford Square London and the sea mist shrouded green of Bedford Square Brighton.

Our goal is to discover irresistible stories and voices that illuminate our world.

We are passionate about connecting our authors to readers across the globe and our independence allows us to do this in original and nimble ways.

The team at Bedford Square Publishers has years of experience and we aim to use that knowledge and creative insight, alongside evolving technology, to reach the right readers for our books. From the ones who read a lot, to the ones who don't consider themselves readers, we aim to find those who will love our books and talk about them as much as we do.

We are hunting for vital new voices from all backgrounds – with books that take the reader to new places and transform perceptions of the world we live in.

Follow us on social media for the latest Bedford Square Publishers news.

@bedsqpublishers
facebook.com/bedfordsq.publishers
@bedfordsq.publishers

bedfordsquarepublishers.co.uk